A Story a Day

365
Stories and Rhymes
for
Girls

Illustrated by Eva Musynski, Marina le Ray, Veronica Vasylenko and Hannah Wood.

Additional illustrations by Simone Abel, Maddy Bell, Alex Burnett, Caroline Jayne Church, Jacqueline East, Chris Embleton, Frances Evans, June Goulding, Anna C. Leplar, Sanja Rescek, Kirsten Richards, Kristina Stephenson, Sara Walker and Michelle White.

Written by Cecil Frances Alexander, William Allingham, Hans Christian Andersen, Kay Barnes, Tina Barrett, William Blake, Jane Euphemia Brown, Moira Butterfield, Deborah Chancellor, Andy Charman, Nick Ellsworth, Gaby Goldsack, Jillian Harker, Karen Hayles, Liz Holliday, Thomas Hood, Lizzie Irvin, John Keats, Charles Kingsley, Edward Lear, Ingrid Maitland, Susan Nicholson, Beatrice Phillpotts, Ronne Randall, Sandy Ransford, Caroline Repchuck, Debbie Rivers-Moore, Beth Roberts, William Roscoe, Christina Rossetti, Anna Sewell, William Shakespeare, Louisa Somerville, Robert Louis Stevenson, Christine Tagg, Jane Taylor, Alfred, Lord Tennyson and Gordon Volke.

Every effort has been made to acknowledge the contributors to this book. If we have made any errors, we will be pleased to rectify them in future editions.

This edition published by Parragon in 2010

Parragon
Queen Street House
4 Queen Street
Bath BA1 1HE, UK

ISBN 978-1-4075-1387-4

Printed in China

A Story a Day

365

Stories and Rhymes

for
Girls

PaRRagon

Bath · New York · Singapore · Hong Kong · Cologne · Delhi · Melbourne

Contents

Contents

Contents

Contents

The Football Fairy

Georgina loved to play football. But there was just one problem.

"I'm fed up with these silly wings," she said one day after a game, wiggling her shoulders. "They just get in the way."

"Flying is brilliant! Anyway, football is a game for elves, not fairies!" said her friend Sparkle.

"In that case, I don't want to be a fairy!" said Georgina, and stamped off.

"She'll change her mind," said Sparkle to herself. "Just wait and see."

The next time Georgina played football, the game was very rough. One elf kicked the ball so hard it flew high into a tree overhanging the pitch and hit a birds' nest – with an egg in it!

The egg tipped... teetered... and began to topple, but none of the elves noticed. They were far too busy arguing with the referee about who had fouled whom.

Just in time, Georgina glanced up and spotted the egg falling from the nest. She caught the egg before it hit the ground. Then she flew back up to the nest.

"Thank you," said the mummy bird, tucking the egg back under her. "But please, be more careful when you play football!"

Next time she played football,

Georgina checked the tree first. The mummy bird was away. "Good!" she thought. "She can't complain this time."

But, thanks to a naughty elf, the football knocked into the birds' nest once again. A small bundle of feathers tumbled out. It was a baby bird!

Georgina spotted it and, quick as lightning, flew up to catch him. Gently, she held him in her arms and flew back to the nest. When he was safely inside she sprinkled him with fairy dust to keep him from further harm.

Just then the mummy bird came back.

"I shall tell everyone about your kindness," she said, when Georgina explained what had happened. "And, as you're such a good fairy, will you be baby Beak's godmother?"

"Oh, thank you! I'd be delighted!" said Georgina.

When they heard the news, the other fairies were very proud of her.

"Perhaps it's not so bad being a fairy after all," grinned Georgina, happily. "But I'm still going to play football!"

One Snowy Day

One snowy day, Old Bear poked his nose out of his den and saw the deep snow that had fallen while he slept.

"I'll take a stroll in the woods," he said. Off he went, his great paws padding along. How he loved the snow! He loved the way it crunched under his feet. Old Bear walked far into the woods, and quite forgot to look where he was going.

After a while, Old Bear stopped. "I'll just take a rest," he said to himself. "I'm not quite sure where I am, but I can follow my pawprints home."

He closed his eyes, and soon fell fast asleep. Meanwhile, the snow started to fall again... and by the time Old Bear woke up his trail of pawprints had disappeared!

"Now I'll never find my way home!" he groaned. Then he noticed an old tree stump nearby.

"That looks familiar. And so does that fallen log over there. If I'm not mistaken, I've walked in a big circle, and ended up at home!" he chuckled, turning towards his den. "What a clever old bear I am, after all!"

Elsie Elephant's Jungle Shower

There wasn't a cloud in the sky, and Elsie Elephant was feeling very hot.

"It's even hot in the shade," she grumbled. "I think I'll go to the river to cool off!"

Tommy Monkey was swinging high up in the tree-tops. "I'm going swimming," Elsie told him. "You can come too, if you like."

"You've got a very long trunk," said Tommy as they wandered towards the river. "What's it for?"

Elsie thought for a minute. "I'm not really sure," she said.

At the river they found Leo Lion standing at the edge of the water, looking in.

"Are you coming for a swim?" asked Elsie.

"Big cats don't swim," sighed Leo. "But I'm so hot!" He watched as Elsie and Tommy splashed into the river.

Elsie saw how hot Leo looked. She looked at her trunk – and had an idea! Filling her trunk with water, she sprayed it all over Leo.

"Thanks, Elsie. This is great!" said Leo.

"*Now* I know what my long trunk is for!" laughed Elsie.

There Was an Old Man from Peru

There was an old man from Peru
Who dreamed he was eating his shoe.
He woke in a fright
In the middle of the night
And found it was perfectly true.

I Eat My Peas with Honey

I eat my peas with honey,
I've done it all my life,
It makes the peas taste funny,
But it keeps them on my knife.

Haymaking

The maids in the meadow
Are making the hay,
The ducks in the river
Are swimming away.

The Old Woman's Three Cows

There was an old woman who had three cows,
Rosy and Colin and Dun.
Rosy and Colin were sold at the fair,
And Dun broke her heart in a fit of despair.
So there was an end of her three cows,
Rosy and Colin and Dun.

Sing, Sing

Sing, sing,
What shall I sing?
The cat's run away
With the pudding string!
Do, do,
What shall I do?
The cat's run away
With the pudding too!

To the Snail

Snail, snail, put out
your horns,
And I will give you bread
and barley corns.

The Easter Bunny

The Easter Bunny's in a flap.
He'll never get it done!
Every year, it's just the same.
He's such a hot, cross bun!

He taps upon the hen-house door.
He hopes that they've been busy.
The hens laugh at his worried face.
He's always in a tizzy!

They fill his basket to the brim,
With eggs of every hue.
There's brown and white and speckled ones
And some are even blue!

The busy bunny hops and skips,
All round and round the towns,
To make quite sure the children wake
With smiles and not with frowns!

But what is this? There's one egg left.
He checks his list to see
If anyone has been left out.
"Oh, yes!" he smiles. "It's me!"

Bertha Saves the Day

Bertha Bunny had a shiny nose,
But this she could not mend,
Because her little powder puff
Was at the other end!

One day, the bunnies hopped and skipped
And wandered off to play
Too far into the Wicked Wood,
Then couldn't find their way!

It got so dark, they couldn't tell
Just which way they should go.
Then Bertie spotted Bertha's nose,
All shiny and aglow!

"Bertha's nose will light our way!"
Cried Bertie Bun, with glee.
"Yippeeee!" the other bunnies yelled.
"We'll soon be home for tea!"

Thank You, Kitty

"Kitty," called Cat one day. "I've got a surprise for you."

Kitty bounced over.

"You can have lots of fun with this ball of wool," said Cat.

Soon Kitty was leaping around. "Watch me, Mum!" she shouted.

"Kitty," called Mother Bird. "Please may I have some wool for my nest?"

Kitty looked at Cat. "I won't have anything to play with," she said sadly. "It won't be any fun."

Cat smiled. "It's much more fun to share things," she said.

Kitty and Cat watched the bird tuck the wool into her nest.

"The baby birds like the wool, don't they, Mum?" laughed Kitty. "I like sharing. Who else can I share my wool with?"

"Why don't you ask the rabbits?" said Cat.

"We're having a hopping race," said Little Rabbit. "A piece of wool is just what we need to make a finishing line. Thank you!"

Just then Cat called Kitty over. "I have a surprise for you," she said. "It's a bell from Mother Bird. To thank you for sharing your wool."

"What a lovely present," said Kitty. "Would you like to play with it too, Mum?"

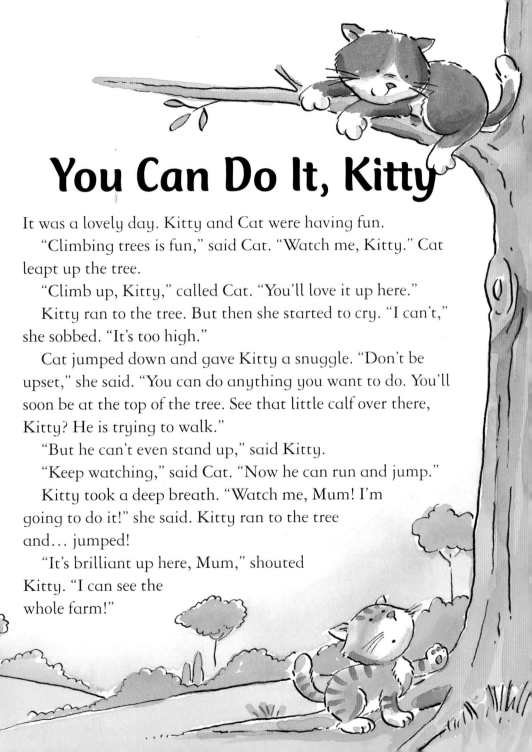

You Can Do It, Kitty

It was a lovely day. Kitty and Cat were having fun.

"Climbing trees is fun," said Cat. "Watch me, Kitty." Cat leapt up the tree.

"Climb up, Kitty," called Cat. "You'll love it up here."

Kitty ran to the tree. But then she started to cry. "I can't," she sobbed. "It's too high."

Cat jumped down and gave Kitty a snuggle. "Don't be upset," she said. "You can do anything you want to do. You'll soon be at the top of the tree. See that little calf over there, Kitty? He is trying to walk."

"But he can't even stand up," said Kitty.

"Keep watching," said Cat. "Now he can run and jump."

Kitty took a deep breath. "Watch me, Mum! I'm going to do it!" she said. Kitty ran to the tree and… jumped!

"It's brilliant up here, Mum," shouted Kitty. "I can see the whole farm!"

The Princess and the Pea

A long time ago, in a land far away, there lived a king and queen who had just one son. The prince was grown up and it was time for him to marry a princess.

"And she must be a real princess," the prince told the king and queen.

But there were no princesses in the land where he lived, so the king and queen arranged for the prince to travel to strange and distant lands to find a bride.

The prince travelled north through frozen lands, until he came to a castle where a princess lived.

This princess was tall and fair and very clever. But she was also vain and boastful.

"A real princess would not be boastful," thought the prince. So he travelled south through hot, sandy deserts, until he came to a palace where a princess lived.

This princess was very beautiful but was also very proud.

"A real princess would not be so proud," thought the prince. And he travelled east through misty lands, until he came to a mansion where a princess lived.

This princess had a charming smile and a lovely voice – but she told the most shocking lies!

"A real princess would never tell lies," thought the prince, so he returned home from his travels, weary, sad and lonely.

One evening, not long after the prince had come home, a terrible storm blew in from the west.

Suddenly, there was a knock at the palace door! The king was so surprised that he went to answer it himself.

There, standing in the windy doorway, was the most bedraggled young woman the king had ever seen.

"Good evening, Your Majesty," she said to the king, curtseying politely. "I am a princess, and I need shelter for the night. May I please come in?"

"Of course," said the king. "We will gladly give you shelter for the night."

When the king told the prince that a princess had turned up at the door, the prince was very eager to meet her. But the queen told him he would have to wait.

"The princess said that she couldn't possibly meet you wet and bedraggled," the queen explained. "She has gone to have a bath and change into some dry clothes."

"That's a good sign," said the prince. "But how can we be

certain that she is a real princess?"

"I have an idea," said his mother. "Leave everything to me."

A short while later, the princess arrived in the main hall dressed in the queen's clothes. Her hair shone, her cheeks were rosy, and her eyes sparkled merrily to match her smile.

The prince and princess sat beside the fire and talked for hours. The prince was enchanted – but he still wasn't sure that the princess was a real princess.

Meanwhile, the queen went to the best guest bedroom carrying a single tiny dried pea.

In the bedroom, she put the pea under the mattress. Then she asked a servant to bring another mattress to put on top of the first, and then another mattress, and another… Until there were *twenty* mattresses on the bed!

Then the queen told the servant to put twenty soft, cosy quilts on top of the mattresses and had a ladder brought for the princess.

The princess was surprised when the queen brought her to the bedroom with its towering bed and ladder. But she didn't protest or complain. She thanked the queen and wished her good night.

The princess climbed the ladder to the very top of the bed. Sighing contentedly, she settled down to sleep. But the princess did not sleep a wink. She tossed and turned all night.

By morning, the princess felt tired and weary. When she came down to breakfast, the prince, the king and the queen greeted her eagerly.

"Did you sleep well?" asked the queen.

"I'm afraid not," sighed the princess. "There was something small and hard in the bed, and no matter which way I turned, I still felt it. I'm dreadfully tired, for I hardly slept at all."

"I'm so sorry," said the queen. "But I'm delighted, too! For this proves that you are indeed a real princess! Only a real princess would feel a tiny pea under twenty mattresses and twenty quilts!"

The prince was overjoyed, for he had already fallen in love with the princess – and she had fallen in love with him. And so they were married.

And what happened to the pea? It was put on a velvet cushion in a glass case, and sent to the museum, where it is still on display today!

Roses Are Red

Roses are red,
Violets are blue,
Sugar is sweet
And so are you.

Little Poll Parrot

Little Poll Parrot
Sat in his garret
Eating toast and tea;
A little brown mouse
Jumped into the house,
And stole it all away.

I Had a Little Horse

I had a little horse,
His name was Dappled Grey,
His head was made of gingerbread,
His tail was made of hay.
He could amble, he could trot,
He could carry the mustard pot,
He could amble, he could trot,
Through the old town of Windsor.

The Legacy

My father died a month ago
And left me all his riches;
A feather bed, a wooden leg,
And a pair of leather breeches;
A coffee pot without a spout,
And a cup without a handle,
A tobacco pipe without a lid,
And half a farthing candle.

Sowing Corn

One for the mouse
One for the crow,
One to rot,
One to grow.

Small Is the Wren

Small is the wren,
Black is the rook,
Great is the sinner
That steals this book.

Jade and the Jewels

Jade was the prettiest mermaid in the lagoon. Her jet-black hair reached right down to the tip of her swishy, fishy tail. Her eyes were as green as emeralds, and her skin was as white as the whitest pearl. And she knew it!

"That Jade thinks too much of herself!" the other mermaids would say. "One of these days she'll come unstuck."

Only one creature was fond of Jade. Gentle the giant turtle followed her wherever she went. But Jade didn't notice Gentle. She lived in her own world, spending all her time combing her hair and looking in the mirror.

One day Jade overheard the other mermaids talking about a pirate ship that had sunk to the bottom of the ocean. On board was a treasure chest filled with precious jewels. "But no one dares take the jewels," whispered the mermaids, "because the pirate ship is cursed!"

"I'm going to find that pirate ship," Jade thought. "Just imagine how beautiful I will look wearing all those jewels!" She set off right away.

Jade swam to a deep part of the ocean she had never been to before. She swam down and down until she found the shipwreck.

She saw the treasure chest through a porthole. Jade swam

inside and reached out to touch
the chest. The lid sprang open and
brilliant jewels spilled over the sides.

Jade lifted out a necklace and put it
round her neck. There was a little gold
and silver mirror in the chest. She held
it up to admire her reflection. It was
beautiful! Jade looked lovelier than
ever.

Suddenly, there was a loud crack
and the mirror shattered. The necklace turned to stone around
her neck – it was the ship's curse! Jade tried to swim, but the
necklace was so heavy she couldn't move.

"Help!" Jade cried out. "Help! Help!"

Gentle the giant turtle had followed Jade down to the
shipwreck. He heard her and swam to the porthole.

"Help me, Gentle," cried Jade, when she saw him. "Please
help me!"

Gentle's powerful flippers broke the necklace and freed Jade.
As they swam away from the wreck, Gentle said, "You don't
need fancy jewels, Jade. You're pretty without
them."

Once she was safely home, Jade told
the other mermaids that the story
about the curse was true.

"And I've learned my lesson," said
Jade. "I'll never be vain again."

Bella Bunny's Bonnet

In pretty Primrose Wood there was great excitement. It was the Spring Parade. All the animals were joining in because prizes were being given for the best bonnets.

"I bet I'll win the prize for the prettiest bonnet," said Bella, who was a very vain bunny. "Now, what can I use to make it?"

She decided to gather some daffodils and bluebells and weave them together.

At the parade Bella looked around at the other animals. "There isn't one hat as pretty as mine," she thought. "It looks good enough to eat!"

Unfortunately Gordy the goat thought so, too. As he trotted behind Bella in the parade, he nibbled away at her bonnet until he had gobbled up nearly all the flowers!

Then Holly the horse gave a loud neigh. "And the winner of the prize for the funniest hat is... Bella Bunny!" she said.

Everyone cheered – except Bella. "But mine isn't funny, it's *beautiful*! Look!" she cried, taking the hat off her head – only to find that it was no more than a pile of twigs!

"Oops!" said Gordy. "Sorry, Bella."

Bella started to laugh. "I guess it serves me right for being so vain," she said. "And I suppose I did win a prize of some sort!"

Brave Billy Bunny

At the edge of Frog Pond Wood lived a friendly little bunny called Billy and his little brother Bobby.

Now the one thing Billy really, really hated was getting wet! So, one sunny day, when the other bunnies and Bobby hopped off to the stream to play, Billy ran through the wood instead, leaping over logs and weaving in and out of the trees. He was very fast!

Suddenly, he heard someone calling his name. It was Bouncer Bunny. "Billy! Come quickly!" he panted. "Bobby's fallen into the deep water and is being washed away!"

Billy rushed off towards the stream, leaving Bouncer far behind. When he reached it, he could just see Bobby in the distance, being quickly washed away downstream.

"Help!" cried Bobby. "I can't swim!"

Then Billy began to run! He managed to get ahead of Bobby. Then he jumped into the water, swam up to his brother and, coughing and spluttering, dragged Bobby to the side.

"Billy!" cried the others. "You're a hero!"

"A wet hero!" said Billy, grinning. "Getting wet wasn't so bad after all. I'm going for another swim – in the shallows!"

Katy and the Butterfly

As Katy Kitten lay dozing happily in the sun,
something tickled her nose. She opened an eye
and saw a butterfly fluttering just above her
whiskers.

Katy sprang after the butterfly, missed
it and landed in a bed of thistles.

"I'll catch that butterfly!" she said,
crossly.

Katy chased the butterfly towards the
stream, where it settled on the branch of a tree.
She climbed after it, but every time she came near, the
butterfly simply flew away – and then she was stuck! She looked
down at the stream swirling below her.

Just then, the butterfly fluttered past her nose. Without
thinking, Katy swiped at it with her paw. But as she did so,
she lost her balance and went tumbling down through the tree,
landing with a great *Splash!* in the water below.

"Help!" cried Katy, waving her paws wildly.
Luckily she caught hold of a branch hanging
over the stream and clambered onto the bank.

Katy arrived home, cold and wet. She curled
up, exhausted, in front of the fire, but just as she
started to doze, she felt something tugging at her
whiskers. She opened one eye and saw a little mouse.

"I've done enough chasing for one day, thank you!" said Katy.

Home Sweet Home

Betty Bunny looked at the sweet green grass growing in the meadow on the far side of the stream. Her mummy had told her never to cross the stream, but she was tired of eating the rough grass that grew near her burrow.

"I'm going to cross the stream!" she said to her brothers and sisters, pointing to a fallen branch that lay across it.

Betty bounced safely across the branch and was soon eating the sweet, juicy grass on the other side of the stream.

"Come over the stream. It's lovely!" she said.

But just then, Betty's brothers and sisters saw a sly fox creeping up behind Betty through the grass!

"Look out!" they called.

Betty turned to see the fox just in time! She leaped back onto the branch, but she was in such a hurry that she slipped and fell into the stream. Luckily, friendly Becky Beaver had been watching and she pulled Betty safely to the other side.

"Home sweet home!" gasped Betty with relief. And she bounced off to join her brothers and sisters, vowing never to leave home again.

Sleepy the Farm Kitten

Sleepy the farm kitten liked nothing better than sleeping all day long, and all through the night. While all the other kittens were busy chasing mice or scaring away birds, he was normally fast asleep.

"Looks too much like hard work to me," he'd yawn, before strolling off to find a comfy spot for a snooze.

One day, while the other kittens were chasing mice around the corn shed, Sleepy stretched and looked around for somewhere to nap.

"You can't sleep here," said the farmer's wife, sweeping Sleepy out of the kitchen. "Today's cleaning day and you'll just be in the way."

"You can't sleep here," mooed the cows, shooing him out of the milking shed. "We're busy being milked, and a kitten can never be trusted around milk."

"You can't sleep here," said the farmer, pushing him out of the dairy. "We're making ice cream and we don't want your hairs all over the place."

"I'm really tired," Sleepy complained to a passing mouse. "Can I sleep with you mice?"

"Don't be ridiculous," laughed the mouse. "Don't you know that kittens are supposed to chase mice?"

Just as Sleepy was about to give up hope of ever finding somewhere to sleep, he spotted the ideal bed – a soft bale of hay sitting on a trailer.

"Purrfect," he purred, curling into a sleepy ball. Within seconds, he was fast asleep.

He was so comfortable that he didn't wake up when the tractor pulling the trailer chugged into life. And he still didn't wake up when the tractor and trailer bumped down the road leading to town.

It was only when the trailer shuddered to a halt that Sleepy woke with a start. He blinked his eyes, stretched, and jumped down. Then he blinked again. He couldn't believe his eyes! He was at market – and the farmer had uncoupled the trailer and was driving away in the tractor.

"Wait for me," mewed Sleepy, leaping down from the trailer. But the farmer had gone.

"I'll have to walk all the way home," thought Sleepy.

Sleepy walked all afternoon and all through the night. The cockerel was just beginning to crow the morning in when he eventually made it back to the farm.

"Hello, lazybones," called the other kittens when they saw him. "Where have you been sleeping all night while we've been chasing mice?"

But for once Sleepy really was tired – far too tired to explain where he had been all night. And it wasn't long before he was fast asleep!

A Hat Like That

Heather the cow took great care of her appearance. She had the shiniest hoofs and the glossiest coat. She had already won three rosettes at the County Show, and she wanted more.

One windy afternoon, when Heather was standing near a hedge, she found a beautiful straw hat on a branch. It had a couple of holes in it, but an elegant cow has to put her ears somewhere!

She strolled back across the field with her nose in the air and the hat placed firmly on her head. Heather couldn't wait to show it off to her friends.

But Poppy, Annabel and Emily simply carried on munching. Heather tried a tiny ladylike cough.

The munching didn't stop for a second. So Heather coughed a little louder. The munching grew louder.

Heather couldn't bear it any longer. "Haven't you noticed it?" she mooed.

"Did I hear something?" asked Emily.

"It was me!" cried Heather, stamping her hoof crossly. "Look at my hat!"

Of course, the other cows had noticed the hat, but they loved to tease their friend.

"I always think,"

said Poppy, "that hats are rather… old-fashioned."

"Nonsense," Heather replied. "Only the most fashionable cows are wearing them."

"It's new then, is it?" asked Annabel.

"Certainly!" Heather replied. "It's the very latest style."

"Didn't Mrs MacDonald have a hat like that a few years ago?" asked Emily.

"I don't think so!" Heather said firmly. "Mrs MacDonald is lovely, but she's not what you would call stylish. Only a prize-winning cow could wear a hat like this."

"If you say so, dear," mooed Annabel.

That evening, the cows ambled into the farmyard to be milked.

Before long, all the other animals had gathered round.

"They're admiring my hat!" whispered Heather to Poppy.

But the giggling and chuckling didn't sound as if they thought Heather looked beautiful. It sounded more like animals who thought she looked rather silly.

"Well, well! So that's what happened to Scarecrow Sam's hat!" cried Old MacDonald.

So nowadays, if Heather starts putting on airs and graces, Poppy, Emily and Annabel know just what to do – they start talking about hats, and Heather tiptoes away.

Ariel's Song

Full fathom five thy father lies;
Of his bones are coral made;
Those are pearls that were his eyes:
Nothing of him that doth fade,
But doth suffer a sea-change
Into something rich and strange:
Sea nymphs hourly ring his knell.
Ding-dong!
Hark! now I hear them,
Ding-dong, bell!

A Frog He Would a-Wooing Go

A frog he would a-wooing go,
Heigho! says Rowley,
Whether his mother would let him or no,
With a rowley, powley, gammon and spinach.

A Candle

Little Nancy Etticoat
In a white petticoat,
And a red rose.
The longer she stands
The shorter she grows.

A Tisket, a Tasket

A tisket, a tasket,
A green and yellow basket.
I wrote a letter to my love,
And on the way I dropped it.
I dropped it, I dropped it,
And on the way I dropped it.
A little girl picked it up
And put it in her pocket.

My Black Hen

Tiggy-tiggy-touchwood, my black hen,
She lays eggs for gentlemen.
Sometimes nine and sometimes ten,
Tiggy-tiggy-touchwood, my black hen.

I Had a Little Hen

I had a little hen, the prettiest ever seen,
She washed me the dishes, and kept the house clean;
She went to the mill to fetch me some flour,
She brought it home in less than an hour;
She baked me my bread, she brewed me my ale,
She sat by the fire and told many a fine tale.

The Naughty Mermaids

Of all the mermaids that lived in the sea, Jazz and Cassandra were the naughtiest. Their latest prank was to swim to the lighthouse, call out to the little boy, Jack, who lived there, and then dive under the waves before he could see them.

One day, Jack's mum had made him a picnic as a treat. Jack laid the food on a cloth on the rocks. He had leftover pizza and crisps and fizzy drinks and chocolate.

The two naughty mermaids popped up from the waves and saw all the food.

"Hello!" they called to Jack. "Are you going to eat all this food by yourself?"

Jack was very surprised. He'd never actually *seen* the mermaids before.

"Yes," said Jack. "I mean, no! You can have some of my picnic, if you like."

The mermaids had never had pizza or crisps or fizzy drink or chocolate before. They ate so much they felt sick!

"Come back tomorrow!" called Jack, who was very excited to have met two *real* mermaids.

King Neptune was angry when he found out what Jazz and Cassandra had been doing. "Mermaids are not children!" he said. "They cannot eat children's food!"

"Humph!" said Cassandra. "I don't believe a word of it. He just wants to stop us having any fun." So the next day the two naughty mermaids swam up to the surface again to meet Jack.

The mermaids ate all Jack's food, then played hide-and-seek in the waves while Jack ran round the lighthouse trying to spot them. They came back the next day and the next. But on the fourth day, when the mermaids said goodbye and started to swim to the bottom of the sea, oh dear! Their tails had become stiff and heavy and they couldn't swim any more!

Jazz and Cassandra clung to the rocks and began to cry.

"What's wrong?" shouted Jack, alarmed.

When the mermaids explained they weren't supposed to eat children's food, Jack knew exactly what to do! He got his net and bucket and collected shrimps and seaweed from the rock pools. For three days and three nights he fed the mermaids mermaid food. By the third day they could move their tails again and swim.

When they arrived home King Neptune was waiting. But this time he wasn't angry – he was glad to see them back safely.

"I hope you two have learned a lesson," he said, quite gently. "Jack has been a good friend so you can play with him again. As long as you don't eat his food!"

Two Princesses

Once upon a time, a long time ago, lived twin princesses called Charmina and Charlotte.

Even though they were twins, they were opposites. Princess Charmina always curtseyed politely to the king and queen. And she remained quite still while the dressmakers came to fit her new ball gown. Princess Charlotte was very different!

"Why do I have to dress like a puffball?" grumbled Princess Charlotte when it was her turn to have a new ball gown fitted.

"How dare you speak to us like that!" her parents cried.

But she did dare. She dared to run barefoot through the gardens. She dared to wear her shabbiest clothes. In fact, she didn't behave like a princess at all!

One day there was to be a ball at the palace. The guests of honour were two princes from the next kingdom.

"Why don't you go for a walk until our guests arrive?" suggested the queen to the two princesses, who were already dressed. "But stay together, don't get dirty and don't be late!"

The princesses walked to the bottom of the palace gardens. "Let's go into the forest," said Princess Charlotte.

"I don't think we should," said Princess Charmina. "Our gowns will get dirty." But Princess Charlotte had already set off.

They hadn't gone far when they heard a strange noise

coming from the next clearing.

"Let's turn back!" said Princess Charmina.

"It might be someone in distress!" said Princess Charlotte. "We have to check!"

They peeped round a tree into the clearing. In it were two horses, but there was no sign of their riders.

Then a voice called out, "Who's there?"

"Look!" said Princess Charmina. In the middle of the clearing there was a deep pit. The princesses crept up to it and peered over the edge. Princess Charmina stared in astonishment. Princess Charlotte burst out laughing. There at the bottom of the pit were the two princes.

"Well, don't just stand there," said the princes. "Get some rope from our saddlebags and help us out!"

The two princesses threw a rope down to the princes and tied the other end to the horses. Soon the princes were rescued.

Everyone enjoyed the ball that evening. The two princesses and two princes danced all night. And from that time on, Charlotte paid more attention to her gowns and hair, while Charmina became a little more playful and daring!

The Littlest Frog

Webster was the littlest frog on Looking-Glass Pond, and every
day he sat on his own, watching the other
frogs play leap-frog over the water.

"Hop it, Titch!" they would croak.
"You're far too small to join in our
games."

"Please let me play with you," said
Webster, one bright, moonlit night. "I can jump really high!"

The other frogs just laughed.

"But I can!" he insisted. He took a deep breath. "I can
jump… over the moon!"

The other frogs laughed so much, they nearly fell off their
lily pads.

"I'll prove it!" he said. "Just watch me."

One… two… three… *jump!* Webster leapt off his lily pad and
sailed over the moon's reflection in the pond.

The other frogs stared in
amazement. It was true. Webster
could jump over the moon!

"We're sorry we didn't believe
you," said one of the big frogs.
"Of course you can play with us.
You might not be the biggest frog
on the pond, but you certainly are
the cleverest!"

Baby Bear's Friend

Baby Bear stretched and took a deep breath of fresh air. He was bursting with energy – all he needed was someone to play with.

"Come and play with me," he called to Owl.

"I only play at night!" said Owl, sleepily.

Nearby some little bunnies were playing. Baby Bear bounded over, but Mrs Rabbit shooed him off. "Your paws will hurt my babies," she said. "You can't play with them."

Baby Bear wandered down to the river, where some beavers were hard at work building a dam.

"Come and play with me," called Baby Bear.

But the beavers were too busy gnawing wood. So he sat watching Kingfisher diving into the water.

"That looks like fun!" he said, jumping in with a splash!

"Go away!" said Kingfisher. "You'll disturb the fish!"

By now Baby Bear was feeling fed up and tired. He lay down and closed his eyes.

Just as Baby Bear was drifting off to sleep, a voice said, "Will you come and play with me?" He opened his eyes to see... another bear cub!

Baby Bear smiled. "I'm too tired to play now," he said. "But I'll play with you tomorrow!"

Don't Be Shy, Suzy

One day Suzy Kitten heard lots of noise
coming from the farmyard.

"What is it, Mum?" she asked.

"There's a big game going on," said Mum.
"It looks fun, doesn't it, Suzy?"

Just then, Parsnip the pig spotted Suzy.
"Hello, Suzy! Come and join in!" he said. But
Suzy hid behind Mum instead.

"What's the matter, Suzy?" asked Mum.

"The game is so loud. It makes me feel
shy," Suzy said sadly.

"There's no need to be shy," said Mum. "It's all your friends
playing the game."

But Suzy still felt shy. "I think I'll just watch," she said.

Then, Dennis the donkey gave the ball a big kick.

"Whoops!" said Dennis. "Did anyone see where the ball went?"

Quick as a flash, Suzy leaped up and scampered up the tree.

"I can see the ball, Mum!" she shouted. "Here it is!"

Suzy threw it down from the tree.

"Thank you, Suzy!" the animals shouted.

The game started again and now Suzy was
right in the middle of things.

"Great kick, Suzy," shouted Parsnip.

"You were right, Mum," Suzy said.

"I didn't need to feel shy at all."

Suzy Helps Out

Suzy and Mum were going for a walk around the farm when Mum heard a noise.

"Someone's crying," she said. "What's the matter, Little Rabbit? Why are you crying?"

"I've lost my teddy bear," sniffed Little Rabbit. "It's my favourite toy."

"Don't worry," said Suzy. "We'll help you look for it. Perhaps it's behind the haystack."

"Well, I can't see your teddy," called Mum. "But here's your ball of wool, Suzy!"

Suzy pointed to the gate. "Perhaps you left your teddy in the field, Little Rabbit," she said.

"I'll never find my teddy," wailed Little Rabbit.

"Don't give up," said Suzy kindly. "I'm sure we'll find it."

"Have you looked for your teddy at home, Little Rabbit?" asked Mum. "It could be there, you know. We've looked everywhere else."

So they walked slowly to Little Rabbit's home, carefully looking for Teddy on the way.

And, when they arrived, they found Teddy, tucked right down inside Little Rabbit's bed!

Little Rabbit gave Suzy a big hug. "Thank you, Suzy and Cat," he said. "I'd never have found my teddy without you!"

Oh, Bear!

There were posters all over town about the circus.

"I think I might join the circus," said Bear to his friend Rabbit.

"What would you do?" asked Rabbit.

"I'd walk the tightrope," said Bear. "It's easy peasy!"

He leapt on to the clothes line and glided gracefully. He somersaulted superbly. He bowed beautifully. Then disaster struck! He wavered and wobbled. He teetered and tottered. He lost his grip and began to slip…

"Oh, Bear!" laughed Rabbit.

"Oh, well," said Bear, as he picked himself up. "Perhaps I'll ride a unicycle instead."

"But you haven't got a unicycle," said Rabbit.

"I can fix that," said Bear. And he disappeared into his shed. Soon, Rabbit heard tools clanging and banging.

"There," called Bear, as he cycled out of the shed.

He pedalled up and down and pirouetted round and round. But then disaster struck!

"Oh, Bear!" laughed Rabbit.

"Oh, well," said Bear, as he picked himself up. "Perhaps I'll juggle instead."

"But there's nothing to juggle," said Rabbit.

"I'll find something," said Bear. And he disappeared into the kitchen. Rabbit waited patiently. He heard crockery clinking and clattering.

"There," said Bear, as he juggled down the path. He whirled the cups and twirled the plates. Higher and higher they went.

Then disaster struck! The cups and plates crashed down and the whole lot smashed.

"Oh, Bear!" laughed Rabbit. "I'm not sure the circus is a good idea."

"Nonsense!" said Bear. "Of course it is."

"But Bear," said Rabbit. "You've tried walking the tightrope. You've tried riding a unicycle. You've tried juggling. And look what happened."

"Yes," said Bear. "Look what happened. I made you laugh. Now I know exactly the right job for me." Quickly he ran indoors.

It wasn't long before he was back.

"Oh, Bear!" laughed Rabbit. "You're right. You make a perfect clown!"

Clumsy Fairy

Clumsy Clementine was the worst in her dance class at Fairy School.

"Clementine! Feathers, not elephants!" Madam Bouquet, the dance teacher, would say.

At the end of term all the fairies were given a special task for the holidays.

"Clementine," said Madam Bouquet, "your job is to paint this rose-petal lotion on a little girl called Alice's spots every night to make them better."

That night Clementine flew in through Alice's window. So far so good! But then clumsy Clementine knocked over a vase...

Alice woke up. "Who's there?" she asked sleepily.

"It's Clementine," said the fairy. She explained why she had come. "You're not really supposed to see me," she added.

"Can you really do magic?" Alice asked Clementine.

"Yes," Clementine told her. "I'm good at magic. But I'm so clumsy!" She told Alice about her dance classes and Alice told Clementine about her ballet lessons.

"I'll help you with your dancing if you like," Alice said to Clementine.

By the end of the week Alice's spots had gone, and Clementine could pirouette.

Madam Bouquet couldn't believe her eyes. "Clementine," she gasped, "what happened?"

"It must be magic!" smiled Clementine.

The Yellow Bluebells

The fairies at Corner Cottage were always busy looking after the flowers in the garden.

It was Blossom's job to paint the bluebells blue.

One evening, Blossom had a cold. "I don't think I can work tonight," she told her friend Petal, sniffing. "I'll have to ask the gnomes."

"No problem!" said Chip and Chuck when she asked them. "Just leave it to us."

When Blossom got up the next morning she was feeling much better – until she saw that the naughty gnomes had painted some of the bluebells… *yellow!*

"Have you seen what they've done?" she said to Petal. "What will Jamie think?"

Jamie lived in Corner Cottage. That morning when he came out to play he noticed that something looked different.

"I'm sure those flowers were blue yesterday," he thought.

"Mum," he said, going into the kitchen, "I've picked you some flowers."

"Yellowbells?" said Mum. "I don't remember planting those."

That night, Blossom painted all the bluebells blue again. When Jamie and his mum went into the garden the next morning, everything was as it should be.

"It must have been fairies!" joked Mum.

Maria's Haircut

One spring day, Maria the sheep stood by the pond in Old MacDonald's farmyard, gazing sadly into the water.

"What is she doing?" whispered Doris the duck to her friend Dora. "You don't often see sheep near water."

Meanwhile, ducklings were swimming across to see who the visitor was.

"Sheep don't eat ducklings, do they?" asked Dora, anxiously.

"Of course not!" replied Doris.

Just then, Maria gave such a big sigh that she blew the ducklings right across the pond and they had to be rescued by their mothers!

"What's the trouble, my dear?" asked Old George, the horse. "Has your lamb run away again?"

"No," sighed Maria. "It isn't that. Just look at me!"

Old George looked carefully at Maria. "Well, you look even more, er, wonderfully woolly than usual," he said, gallantly.

"I look a fright," said Maria. "My coat should have been trimmed weeks ago, but Old MacDonald seems to have forgotten."

"Hmmmm. He can be a little forgetful," said Old George. "I'll speak to the other animals and see what they suggest."

"Perhaps I could nibble her coat," said Percy the pig, who would eat almost anything!

"No, we need to remind Old MacDonald to give Maria a haircut," said Poppy the cow.

"Old MacDonald is always so busy," added Henrietta the hen. "How can we make him notice Maria's problem?"

That gave Poppy a very good idea.

"It's Mrs MacDonald that notices things," she mooed thoughtfully. "Perhaps you *should* do some nibbling, Percy!"

So Percy did a little nibbling and the hens scurried away with the tufts of wool in their beaks, searching for the farmer.

When Old MacDonald went into the farmhouse for his lunch that day, Mrs MacDonald threw up her hands in horror! "MacD!" she cried. "You're covered in wool! Don't bring all those fluffy bits into my clean kitchen! It's obviously time those sheep were shorn."

The very next day, Maria's haircut was the talk of the farmyard. And she and her friends strutted happily around, looking as smart and as stylish as any sheep you've ever seen.

Sunshine

A sunshiny shower
Won't last half an hour.

Mrs Hen

Chook, chook, chook, chook, chook,
Good morning, Mrs Hen.
How many chickens have you got?
Madam, I've got ten.
Four of them are yellow,
And four of them are brown,
And two of them are speckled red,
The nicest in the town.

Thaw

Over the land freckled with snow half-thawed
The speculating rooks at their nests cawed,
And saw from elm-tops, delicate as flower of grass,
What we below could not see, winter pass.

Little Boy Blue

Little Boy Blue, come blow your horn,
The sheep's in the meadow,
The cow's in the corn.
Where is the boy who looks after the sheep?
He's under a haycock fast asleep.
Will you wake him?
No, not I,
For if I do he's sure to cry.

Billy and Me

One, two, three,
I love coffee,
And Billy loves tea,
How good you be,
One two three,
I love coffee,
And Billy loves tea.

Little Nag

I had a little nag
That trotted up and down;
I bridled him, and saddled him,
And trotted out of town.

Sugarplum and the Butterfly

"Sugarplum," said the Fairy Queen, "I've got a very important job for you to do." Sugarplum was always given the most important work. The Fairy Queen said it was because she was the kindest and most helpful of all the fairies. "I want you to make a rose-petal ball gown for my birthday ball next week."

"It will be my pleasure," said Sugarplum happily.

Sugarplum began to gather cobwebs for the thread, and rose petals for the dress. While she was collecting the thread she found a butterfly caught in a cobweb.

"Oh, you poor thing," sighed Sugarplum. Very carefully, she untangled the butterfly, but his wing was broken. Sugarplum laid the butterfly on a bed of feathers. She gathered some nectar from a special flower and fed him a drop at a time. Then she set about mending his wing with a magic spell.

After six days, the butterfly was better. He was very grateful. But now Sugarplum was behind with her work!

"Oh dear! I shall never finish the Fairy Queen's ball gown by tomorrow," she cried. "Whatever shall I do?"

The butterfly comforted her. "Don't worry, Sugarplum," he

said. "We'll help you."

He gathered all his friends together. There were yellow, blue, red and orange butterflies. He told them how Sugarplum had rescued him from the cobweb and helped to mend his wing.

The butterflies gladly gathered up lots of rose petals and dropped them next to Sugarplum. Then the butterflies flew away to gather more cobwebs, while Sugarplum arranged all the petals. Back and forth went Sugarplum's hand with her needle and thread making the finest cobweb stitches. Sugarplum added satin ribbons and bows. When she had finished, Sugarplum was very pleased with the ball gown.

"Dear friend," she said to the butterfly, "I couldn't have finished the dress without your help."

"And I could never have flown again without your kindness and help," said the butterfly.

And the Fairy Queen was delighted with her new ball gown!

The Elves and the Shoemaker

Once upon a time there was a kind old shoemaker. He worked hard, but the day came when he had only a few pennies left – just enough to buy leather for one final pair of shoes.

That evening the shoemaker cut up the leather. Then, leaving it on his workbench, he climbed the stairs to bed.

The next morning the shoemaker couldn't believe his eyes. On his workbench was the finest pair of shoes he had ever seen. He put the shoes in his shop window and that afternoon a fine gentleman bought them for a price that amazed the shoemaker.

The money was enough to buy enough leather to make two new pairs of shoes. The shoemaker cut up the leather and left it lying on his workbench. "I'll finish the shoes tomorrow," he yawned, and went to bed.

The next morning, when he came downstairs, the shoemaker saw two fine pairs of beautiful new shoes!

So it went on for weeks. Every night the shoemaker cut out the leather and left it on his workbench, and every morning there were splendid shoes waiting to be sold.

One night the shoemaker and his wife decided that they had to solve the mystery. So, after the shoemaker left the leather on his workbench, they shut up shop and hid in a cupboard.

When the clock struck midnight, two tiny elves appeared. They ran over to the workbench and began to stitch and sew, until they had made five pairs of shoes. Then they shot up the chimney.

"The elves must be frozen in those thin, tattered clothes," said the shoemaker. "And their feet are bare, although they make such beautiful shoes!"

So the shoemaker's wife made two little jackets and two pairs of trousers. The shoemaker made two pairs of tiny boots, fastened with shiny silver buckles. The next evening, they wrapped the little clothes in tissue paper and left them on the workbench. Then they hid in the cupboard and waited.

At the stroke of midnight, the elves appeared. When they opened the presents, they were overjoyed. They put on their new clothes and danced happily all around the shop, singing,

"See what handsome boys we are!
We will work on shoes no more!"

Then they flew up the chimney and were gone, never to return again! But the shoemaker and his wife never forgot them.

Kiss It Better

Rumpus was romping around the living room. He cartwheeled across the carpet. He turned a somersault on the sofa.

"Be careful!" called Mum. Too late! Rumpus slipped from the sofa and banged his head.

"My head hurts!" he groaned.

"Come here and I'll kiss it better," said Mum. She hugged Rumpus and planted a kiss on his forehead. "Now go and find something less rowdy to do," she said.

Rumpus rushed out into the garden and began to ride his bike. Round and round he raced.

"Watch out!" called Mum. Too late! Rumpus crashed into the corner of the wheelbarrow and grazed his knee.

"My leg hurts!" he wailed.

"Come here and I'll kiss it better," said Mum. She hugged Rumpus and planted a kiss on his knee. "Now go and find something safer to do," she said.

Rumpus ran up the grassy slope. Then he

rolled down. "Roly poly, down the hill," he sang.

"Look where you're going!" called Mum. Too late! Rumpus rolled right into the rose bush. The thorns scratched him all along his arm.

"My arm's sore!" cried Rumpus.

"Come here and I'll kiss it better," said Mum, and she planted kisses all up his arm. "Now, try and keep out of trouble," she said.

Mum went into the kitchen. "I need a break," she thought. She made a cup of tea. She cut herself a slice of cake. Then she sat down for five minutes. Just as she picked up her cup, Rumpus zoomed into the kitchen on his skateboard.

"Rumpus!" said Mum. She moved into the living room. She sat down on the sofa and picked up the paper.

Boom! Boom! Boom! In marched Rumpus, banging on his drum. Mum sighed.

"Is anything wrong?" asked Rumpus.

"I've got a headache!" said Mum.

"Never mind," smiled Rumpus, throwing his arms around her. "I'll soon kiss it better."

Helpful Baby Elephant

"Giraffe, you've lost your patterns in the mud," said Baby Elephant to his friend. "I'll spray you with my trunk."

"Monkey, you look very tired," said Baby Elephant to his friend. "I'll carry you on my back."

"Oh no, Rhino! You've fallen in the river," said Baby Elephant to his friend. "Hold on to my tail. I'll pull you out!"

Soon Baby Elephant needed a rest. He settled down under a tree and closed his eyes. But no sooner had he closed them than he noticed lots of funny noises. Rustlings and warblings and the distant roar of lions. What if a lion was coming to eat him? Baby Elephant was scared! He opened his eyes with a start.

"What's the matter, Baby Elephant?" asked Monkey.

"When I close my eyes, I start to notice lots of noises," explained Baby Elephant. "It makes me scared to go to sleep. What if a lion ate me while I was asleep?"

"Don't worry, Baby Elephant!" said Monkey. "Now it's our turn to help you. Settle down and close your eyes. Your friends will keep you as safe as safe can be while you rest."

"Thank you!" said Baby Elephant.

Sleepy Baby Tiger

Baby Tiger yawned as he followed Mum. It was so hot!

"Keep up!" said Mum to the tiger cubs. "Today we are learning how to use our stripes as camouflage."

Baby Tiger wasn't too sure what camouflage was. And the long grass looked so soft and shady. When Mum wasn't looking, he stepped off the trail, curled up and fell fast asleep.

Baby Tiger was woken a little while later by voices.

"He must be somewhere round here," said Mum's voice.

Baby Tiger felt very guilty. "Here I am," he called nervously.

"You were hiding!" said Mum.

"Camouflaged!" said one of the other cubs. "In the long grass."

"Er... yes," said Baby Tiger uncertainly.

Mum nuzzled Baby Tiger. "Don't hide for that long again," she said. "But that was brilliant camouflage. You used your stripes to hide yourself in the long grass like a grown-up tiger."

Baby Tiger smiled.

"Now follow me!" said Mum. "The next lesson is about how to stalk silently through the trees."

Cuddles to the Rescue

Cuddles was a very smart little poodle. Her hair was snowy white and fell in perfect curls. She wore a crisp red bow on top of her head. And she never went out without her sparkly jewelled collar.

But although Cuddles was the smartest, most pampered pooch around, she was not happy. You see, she didn't have any doggy friends.

Whenever Gilly her owner took Cuddles walking in the park, Cuddles tried her best to make friends, but the other dogs didn't want to know her.

"Here comes Miss Snooty," they would bark. Then they'd point and snigger, before racing away.

And Cuddles was never let off her velvet lead. "Those other dogs look rough," explained Gilly. "You're safer with me."

Cuddles would have loved to run around with the other dogs. She thought that chasing sticks and balls looked like brilliant fun. And she was sure that she'd be able to swim in the lake if only Gilly would let her.

But the other dogs didn't know that Cuddles wanted to be one of them. They just took one look at her snowy white curls and sparkly collar and thought that she was too posh for them.

"She doesn't want to get her paws dirty," Mrs Collie

explained to Skip, her youngest pup, when he asked why Cuddles was always on a lead.

One day, Cuddles was walking with Gilly in the park when she saw Skip chasing ducks beside the lake.

"Careful!" barked Cuddles, as Skip bounced up and down excitedly. But Skip was far too busy to listen. Then Skip took an extra large bounce... into the lake!

"Help, help!" barked Skip, as he splashed about wildly in the lake. Cuddles gave a loud bark, and then, using all her strength, pulled the lead from Gilly's hand.

Cuddles was in the water in an instant. Gilly looked on in horror as Cuddles pulled the struggling pup ashore.

Once on dry land, Cuddles gave herself a big shake, then started to lick Skip dry.

"You were so brave, Cuddles!" cried Gilly.

"Will you play with me?" barked Skip, wagging his tail hopefully.

After that, Gilly always let Cuddles play with the other dogs in the park, and Cuddles was the happiest little poodle around.

Hurt No Living Thing

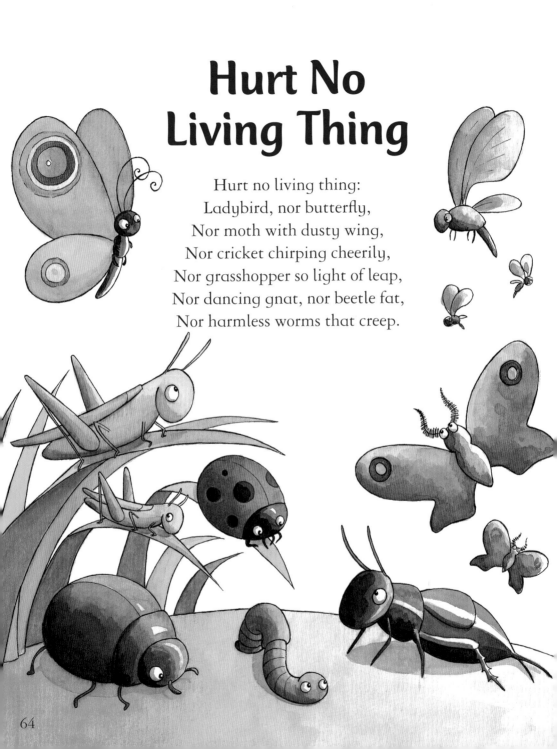

Hurt no living thing:
Ladybird, nor butterfly,
Nor moth with dusty wing,
Nor cricket chirping cheerily,
Nor grasshopper so light of leap,
Nor dancing gnat, nor beetle fat,
Nor harmless worms that creep.

The Great Brown Owl

The brown owl sits in the ivy-bush,
And she looketh wondrous wise,
With a horny beak beneath her cowl,
And a pair of large, round eyes.

She sat all day on the selfsame spray,
From sunrise till sunset;
And the dim grey light, it was all too bright
For the owl to see in yet.

"Jenny Owlet, Jenny Owlet," said a merry little bird,
"They say you're wondrous wise;
But I don't think you see, though you're looking at me
With your large, round, shining eyes."

But night came soon, and the pale white moon
Rolled high up in the skies;
And the great brown owl flew away in her cowl,
With her large, round, shining eyes.

Mousie

Mousie comes a-creeping, creeping.
Mousie comes a-peeping, peeping.
Mousie says, "I'd like to stay, but I haven't time today."
Mousie pops into his hole
And says, "*Achoo!* I've caught a cold!"

Mrs Mason's Basin

Mrs Mason bought a basin,
Mrs Tyson said, "What a nice one,"
"What did it cost?" asked Mrs Frost,
"Half a crown," said Mrs Brown,
"Did it indeed," said Mrs Reed,
"It did for certain," said Mrs Burton.
Then Mrs Nix, up to her tricks,
Threw the basin on the bricks.

Ride a Cock-Horse

Ride a cock-horse to Banbury Cross,
To see a fine lady ride on a white horse,
Rings on her fingers and bells on her toes,
She shall have music wherever she goes.

Grandma's Glasses

These are Grandma's glasses,
This is Grandma's hat;
Grandma claps her hands like this,
And rests them in her lap.

These are Grandpa's glasses,
This is Grandpa's hat;
Grandpa folds his arms like this,
And has a little nap.

Tickly, Tickly

Tickly, tickly, on your knee,
If you laugh, you don't love me.

Build a House with Five Bricks

Build a house with five bricks,
One, two, three, four, five.
Put a roof on top,
And a chimney too,
Where the wind blows through!

Little Red Riding Hood

There was once a little girl who lived with her mother at the edge of a forest. She was kind and sweet, and everyone loved her. The little girl often wore a red velvet cape with a hood. So everyone called her Little Red Riding Hood.

One day, Little Red Riding Hood's mother put some cake and fruit in a basket.

"This is for Granny," Mother told Little Red Riding Hood. "She isn't feeling well, and these goodies will cheer her up."

"Can I take the goodies to her?" asked Little Red Riding Hood. Her granny lived on the other side of the forest.

"Of course," said Mother. "But you must promise to be very careful. Stay on the path, and don't speak to *any* strangers!"

"I promise, Mother," said Little Red Riding Hood, and off she went.

As Little Red Riding Hood skipped along the path through the forest, she didn't know that a sly, greedy old wolf was watching her!

A little way down the path, the wolf sprang out in front of her.

"Good morning, my dear!" said the wolf, with a big, toothy grin.

Little Red Riding Hood remembered

what her mother had told her, and she didn't speak to the wolf. She kept walking. But that sly old wolf just followed her!

"Where are you going on this fine morning?" the wolf asked.

Not wanting to be rude, Little Red Riding Hood answered, "To my granny's house, on the other side of the forest, sir. She isn't feeling well, and I'm taking some goodies to cheer her up."

"Hmm," the wolf thought to himself. "This little girl might make a sweet snack, but her granny would make a tasty meal!" He began to work out a crafty plan.

"Wouldn't your granny like some pretty flowers?" the wolf asked Little Red Riding Hood.

"Yes, Granny loves flowers," said Little Red Riding Hood, and she began to gather flowers. She strayed further and further into the forest, forgetting her mother's warning.

Meanwhile, the wolf hurried straight to Granny's house. He knocked on the door.

"Who's there?" called Granny.

"It's Little Red Riding Hood," called the wolf, in his softest, sweetest voice.

"Just open the door and come in," said Granny.

So the wolf opened the door and went right in.

Before poor Granny knew what had happened, the wolf had gobbled her up in one big gulp.

Then the wolf put on Granny's

nightcap and crept into her bed.

Soon, Little Red Riding Hood arrived at the cottage with a posy of flowers. She knocked on the door.

"Who's there?" called the wolf in his gentlest granny voice.

"It's Little Red Riding Hood."

"Just open the door and come in," said the wolf.

So Little Red Riding Hood opened the door and went right in.

Little Red Riding Hood looked over at the bed.

"Poor Granny must be very ill," she thought. "She looks so strange!" Little Red Riding Hood stepped closer to the bed.

"Oh, Granny!" she gasped. "What big eyes you have!"

"All the better to see you with, my dear," said the wolf.

"Oh, Granny!" she said. "What big ears you have!"

"All the better to hear you with, my dear," said the wolf.

"Oh, Granny, what big hands you have!"

"All the better to hold you with!" said the wolf.

"Oh, Granny!" she said. "What big teeth you have!"

"All the better to eat you with!" growled the wolf, jumping out of bed. And he gobbled up Little Red Riding Hood in one big gulp!

With his belly so full it was almost ready to burst, the wolf lay back down on the bed and fell fast asleep.

At that moment, a hunter was passing Granny's cottage, and he heard a strange sound coming through the open window.

"The poor old woman is snoring very loudly!" the hunter said to himself. "I'd better go in and see if she's all right."

So, in went the hunter. Of course he saw that it wasn't Granny who was snoring at all – it was the wolf!

"I have been hunting you for a long time," he cried. "Now, at last, I have found you!" He raised his gun to shoot the wolf. But then he looked at the wolf's belly.

"You sly old wolf!" cried the hunter. "From the size of your belly, I'd say you've swallowed poor old Granny!"

He took out his hunting knife and very carefully slit open the wolf's belly – zip, zip!

Out jumped Granny – and Little Red Riding Hood, too!

"Thank you for saving us!" said Granny.

While the wolf was still asleep, Little Red Riding Hood went outside and got some stones. She brought them in and filled the wolf's belly with them. Then the hunter stitched up the wolf's belly as good as new.

When the wolf woke up a little while later, he had such a bellyache that he ran out of the cottage moaning and groaning. He went off to hide in a cave, and was never, ever seen again!

Two Little Kittens

Two little kittens, one stormy night,
Began to quarrel, and then to fight;
One had a mouse, the other had none,
And that's the way the quarrel began.

"I'll have that mouse," said the biggest cat;
"You'll have that mouse? We'll see about that!"
"I will have that mouse," said the eldest son;
"You shan't have the mouse," said the little one.

I told you before 'twas a stormy night
When these two little kittens began to fight.
The old woman seized her sweeping broom,
And swept the kittens right out of the room.

The ground was covered with frost and snow,
And the two little kittens had nowhere to go.
So they laid them down on the mat at the door,
While the old woman finished sweeping the floor.

Then they crept in, as quiet as mice,
All wet with snow, and cold as ice,
For they found it was better, that stormy night,
To lie down and sleep than to quarrel and fight.

Princess Sleepyhead

Goodnight, Princess Sleepyhead!
It's time to climb the stairs to bed.
Tidy up. There's lots of mess!
Neatly hang your pretty dress.

Brush your teeth. Make sure they're clean.
Brush up and down until they gleam!
Put your jewels in their box.
Brush your long and silky locks.

Snuggle down, switch on your light.
It shines just like the stars at night.
Sleep tight beneath its cosy beams –
Goodnight, Princess. Have sweet dreams!

Slow Down, Bruce

On Old MacDonald's farm, no one works harder than Bruce the farm dog – except, of course, Old MacDonald! All day long, Bruce dashes around the farm, keeping an eye on everything that goes on. So, when Bruce stayed in his kennel one morning with his head on his paws, everyone began to worry.

"It's not like him at all," clucked Henrietta the hen.

"He can hardly open his eyes," purred Milly the cat.

"I've never known him have a day's illness in his life," said Old George the horse, "and I remember him as a pup."

Old MacDonald was more worried than any of them.

"Just stay there, old boy," he said gently. "I'll get someone to help you." And he hurried off to call the vet.

The vet arrived very quickly. She too was very fond of Bruce. She carefully examined him, lifting his paws one by one, and checking every part of him thoroughly. Then she patted the old dog's head and said, "You're like your master. You need to stop dashing around so much and take better care of yourself. You'll be fine in a day or two, but just slow down, Bruce. Take it easy for once, please."

Bruce nodded his head gratefully and went back to sleep.

Now, Mrs MacDonald had been listening, and returned to the farmhouse with a thoughtful look on her face.

Bruce did as he was told, and by the end of the week he was as right as rain – it would soon be time to go back to work.

When he saw Old MacDonald rushing through the yard, hurrying to finish a job, Bruce dashed after him.

But Mrs MacDonald rushed out of the farmhouse and called to the farmer.

"Husband!" she cried. "Did you hear what the vet said about Bruce? You must set him a good example! Please be a little more thoughtful!"

So Old MacDonald began to slow down, and so did Bruce. The sheepdog soon felt better for it – and so did Old MacDonald. And Mrs MacDonald, who had been begging her husband to take it easy for years, felt very happy indeed.

Harvey the Shyest Rabbit

Harvey the rabbit was the shyest animal in the glade beside Looking-Glass Pond. He was too shy to talk to anyone... too shy to play with the other animals... too shy even to look out from behind his big floppy ears.

"There's no need to be scared," Mamma Rabbit told him. "If you want to join in, all you have to do is ask."

But Harvey just hid behind the long grass. No one even noticed that he was there!

One morning, Harvey was sitting beside Looking-Glass Pond – alone, as usual.

"I wish I could make a friend," he sighed. "But how can I,

when no one even notices me?"

Harvey gazed down sadly at the pond. He could hardly believe his eyes! There in the water was another little rabbit with big floppy ears, staring back at him.

"He looks just as scared as me!" thought Harvey.

He waved shyly at the rabbit in the water. The water rabbit waved too! Harvey did a bunny hop in surprise. The water rabbit did a bunny hop.

"Hello!" said Harvey bravely, smiling.

"Hello!" said the rabbit, smiling back.

"So that's how you make friends!" cried Harvey, in amazement. "You just need to be a little bit brave."

He was so excited, he forgot all about being shy or scared. Instead, he raced off to tell everyone the good news.

And this time, everyone noticed him! Soon Harvey had lots of new friends to play with. But he never forgot to visit his very first friend in Looking-Glass Pond!

Small and Pink

One morning, Percy the pig strutted proudly through the farmyard.

"Today's the day," he told everyone he passed.

"What is he on about?" asked Doris the duck.

"Percy is expecting some piglets," clucked Jenny the hen.

"I didn't think boy pigs could have babies," said Doris, looking puzzled.

"No, no," Jenny clucked, flapping her wings. "They are coming from another farm to live here as part of his family."

Percy had tripped and trotted from one end of the farmyard to the other more times than he cared to remember, but Farmer Brown still hadn't returned with the new arrivals.

Percy went back to his sty and checked it one more time. It was spotless. The straw was piled up neatly along one wall and the water trough was clean and full.

"I must make sure that everything is ready for my piglets," said Percy, brushing a speck of dust from the doorway.

Just as Percy finished cleaning, brushing and tidying he heard Farmer Brown's truck rumbling into the farmyard – they were here at last!

Percy was so excited! He hurried from his sty, but before he could reach the truck…

Whoosh! Something very small, very pink and very fast shot past his nose.

Whizzz! Something just as small and pink and even faster

scuttled under his tail.

Wheeeee! Another small and pink and noisy thing zoomed straight under Percy's tummy.

"*Eeeeeeeeee!*" shrieked seven little piglets, dashing in every direction around the farmyard.

Late that night, a very tired Percy stood at the doorway of his sty – it was a tip. The straw was everywhere and the water trough was upside down. But seven little piglets were fast asleep in the corner.

"They never stand still, do they?" said Jasmine the sheep.

"No," sighed Percy.

"Are you having second thoughts, Percy?" asked Old Harry the horse.

But Percy gave the kind of grin that only a very happy, contented and proud pig can give. "*Shhhhhhh!*" he whispered. "My babies are sleeping!"

The Emperor's New Clothes

Once upon a time there was an emperor who loved new clothes. Every morning, the emperor swept through the palace in brand-new clothes, enjoying the admiration of everyone he met.

One day, the emperor told the chief minister to organize a grand parade.

"It will be a wonderful opportunity to show off a splendid new outfit!" said the emperor. "Find me the very best tailors and the very finest cloth in the kingdom!"

"Yes, Your Majesty," said the chief minister dutifully. He sent messengers to every corner of the land.

Two rascals heard the message about the emperor's parade. They hatched a cunning plan.

A queue of tailors soon appeared at the palace doors, with magnificent rolls of rich fabrics. But at the head of the queue stood two tailors who seemed to have nothing at all.

"We have something very special to show the emperor," said the two tailors. "Something no one has ever seen before."

Impressed, the chief minister ushered them into the palace. The tailors stood before the emperor, holding out their arms.

"This, Your Majesty," said the first man, "is the most amazing cloth in the whole world."

"It is invisible," said his companion, "but only to fools and simpletons. Anyone with wisdom can see how beautiful it is."

Of course, the emperor could not see anything – because there was nothing there! The tailors were actually the two cunning cheats, who had come to trick him.

Not wanting to look like a fool, the emperor said, "Yes, this cloth is magnificent." He immediately ordered a new outfit made of the splendid cloth. A workshop was set up for the two cunning rascals. They asked for payment in advance, so the emperor gave them a purse filled with coins.

"We will need a loom and the finest gold thread in the kingdom," they told the emperor.

When the loom and thread arrived, the two tailors set to work. Hiding the gold thread in their knapsacks, they began to 'weave'. But of course, the loom was empty!

The next day, the two tailors came to measure the emperor for his new outfit. One busied himself with the tape measure, while the other spoke to the chief minister.

"We will need more cloth than we thought," said the first tailor. "We must have more money and more gold thread."

"Of course," said the chief minister, handing over another bulging purse.

For the next few days and nights, the two rascals stayed in their workshop with the doors locked.

As the day of the parade drew near, the emperor grew anxious. He told his chief minister to check on the tailors.

The two cunning rascals refused to let the chief minister in.

"It will spoil the surprise," they told him. "But if you give us more money, we can finish the suit sooner."

The chief minister handed over another purse filled with coins, then went back to the emperor.

"The new suit is beautiful," he told the emperor.

The day of the parade arrived, and the tailors were summoned. As the emperor undressed, the tailors pretended to hand him his new clothes. And the emperor carefully pretended to put them on.

As the emperor strode proudly through the palace corridors, the palace courtiers and servants bowed and murmured words of praise. They all knew that the clothes were only invisible to fools and simpletons, and no one wanted to be thought a fool!

A huge crowd gathered to watch the grand parade.

Everyone wanted to know if their friends and neighbours were simple fools who couldn't see the emperor's new clothes.

At last the royal procession came into view. A fanfare of trumpets announced that the emperor was coming.

A gasp rose from the crowd, quickly followed by cheers.

"Look at the emperor's beautiful new clothes!" people cried.

At the back of the crowd, one little boy hopped up and down to see the emperor's magnificent new clothes. He pushed his way to the front of the crowd.

"The emperor has no clothes on!" he cried, pointing and laughing. The crowd fell silent. Then someone called out, "The boy is right! It's true – the emperor has no clothes on!"

Soon everyone in the crowd was saying it: "The emperor has no clothes on!" "The emperor has no clothes on!"

The emperor knew that they were right. He blushed with embarrassment. "I didn't want anyone to think I was a fool," he thought, "but I have turned out to be the biggest fool of all."

And so the emperor just kept walking, staring straight ahead. He didn't see the two cunning rascals sneak away, laughing and clutching their bags of gold.

Little Miss Muffet

Little Miss Muffet
Sat on a tuffet,
Eating her curds and whey;
There came a big spider,
Who sat down beside her,
And frightened Miss Muffet away.

Little Jumping Joan

Here am I, little jumping Joan.
When nobody's with me,
I'm always alone.

There Was a Little Girl

There was a little girl, and she had a little curl
Right in the middle of her forehead;
When she was good she was very, very good,
But when she was bad she was horrid.

Anna Maria

Anna Maria she sat on the fire;
The fire was too hot, she sat on the pot;
The pot was too round, she sat on the ground;
The ground was too flat, she sat on the cat;
The cat ran away with Maria on her back.

Round-eared Cap

A pretty little girl in a round-eared cap
I met in the streets the other day;
She gave me such a thump,
That my heart it went bump;
I thought I should have fainted away!
I thought I should have fainted away!

Goldy Locks, Goldy Locks

Goldy locks, goldy locks,
Wilt thou be mine?
Thou shall not wash dishes,
Nor yet feed the swine;

But sit on a cushion,
And sew a fine seam,
And feed upon strawberries,
Sugar and cream.

I Love My Puppy

I love my puppy because he wags his tail,
When he comes to meet me it wags without fail!
He barks and jumps when he wants to play,
He'd like to chase my bouncy ball all of the day.

He fetches me sticks to throw for him.
(If they fall into the pond then he'll go for a swim!)
He scampers beside me when we walk in the park,
When he sees other dogs he just *loves* to bark.

But I love him most of all when the day is done,
And we snuggle up close after having fun.

I Love My Kitten

I love my kitten because of her purr,
She purrs so softly when I stroke her fur!
She loves to pounce upon a ball of wool,
And use her paws to roll, tumble and pull.

She washes her face by licking her paws,
She does *try* not to scratch me with her claws,
She peeps through the cat flap to see if dinner's there,
And if it isn't she miaows to make me aware!

But I love her most of all when she just sits and purrs,
With her tail curled all around her.

I Love My Pony

I love my pony because he neighs hello to me,
When he gallops through the meadows he looks so free,
He lets me sponge him and brush his soft shiny mane,
He'll go for a ride in the sun, wind or rain.

He jumps at the show and wins lots of rosettes.
(Though we haven't won a first-place one yet.)
He's fun to be with when we go for long rides,
When he canters beautifully I'm filled with pride.

But I love him most of all when we stand very close,
And he nuzzles me with his velvet-soft nose.

I Love My Bunny

I love my bunny because he twitches his nose,
He twitches it especially when the wind blows!
When he runs in the garden his fluffy white tail
Bobs up and down as he follows a trail.

He nibbles carrots with his bright white teeth,
And digs holes in the lawn to see what's beneath.
(If Mum's watching when he does that she usually shouts,
I don't really know what the problem's about.)

But I love him most of all when he sits on my lap,
And I stroke his big floppy ears and he has a nap.

The Ugly Duckling

One sunny summer day, a mother duck built her nest among the reeds near the moat of an old castle. There she laid her eggs, and there she sat, keeping them warm, day after day.

Finally, the eggs began to crack. *Peep! Peep!* Out popped each fuzzy little duckling's head, one after another.

Then Mother Duck noticed that one last egg, the biggest one of all, had not yet hatched. She carried on sitting on it. Days later, the biggest egg began to crack.

"*Honk! Honk!*" said the duckling. He was much bigger and scruffier than the other ducklings.

"He's not as pretty as my other babies," Mother Duck said to herself. "But I'll look after him, just the same."

The next morning, Mother Duck took all her babies for their first swimming lesson. They followed her into the water, one by one. They all swam beautifully – and the big, ugly duckling swam best of all!

The other ducks came to watch.

"Who's that scruffy creature?" squawked one.

"He's my youngest duckling," said Mother Duck. "See how well he swims!"

"But he's so big and so *ugly!*" quacked the other ducks, laughing.

That afternoon, Mother Duck took all her ducklings to the farmyard.

As soon as the farmyard animals saw the ugly duckling, they began to laugh and shout.

"Most of your ducklings are lovely," clucked the hen. "But look at that big, scruffy, *ugly* one!"

"He's too ugly for this farmyard!" cackled the goose.

The same thing happened the next day, and the day after that. The ducks on the moat and the animals in the farmyard all teased the ugly duckling. Even his own brothers and sisters made fun of him. The ugly duckling had no friends at all.

The ugly duckling was so sad and lonely that he decided to run away, out into the big, wide world.

Early one morning, before anyone else was awake, he ran away, through the reeds, past the moat and the farmyard and the castle walls, till he came to a marsh.

There he saw a flock of wild ducks dabbling in the water.

"What kind of bird are you?" they asked.

"I'm a duckling," the ugly duckling replied.

"No, you're not," said the biggest duck. "You're much too ugly! We don't want to have anything to do with you!" And they turned away, leaving him alone.

The ugly duckling spent two lonely days on the marsh, until a group of hunters came, scaring all the ducks away.

The frightened ugly duckling ran over fields and meadows. He wandered far and wide until he came to a lake where he could swim and find food. There were other ducks there, but when they saw how ugly he was, they kept far away from him.

The ugly duckling stayed on the lake all summer. Then the autumn came, and the weather began to grow cold. All the other ducks began to fly south, where the weather was warmer. The ugly duckling shivered by himself in the tall grass beside the lake.

One evening, just before sunset, the ugly duckling looked up and saw a flock of big, beautiful birds above him. Their white feathers gleamed and they had long, graceful necks. They were flying south, just like the ducks.

The ugly duckling stretched his neck to watch them.

"I wish I could go with them," he thought.

Autumn turned to winter, and the lake froze solid. The ugly duckling couldn't swim any longer. His feathers were caked with ice and snow, and he couldn't find any food.

Luckily, a farmer found the ugly duckling and took him home. The farmer's wife warmed the ugly duckling up by the stove, and the farmer's children tried to play with him. But they were loud and rough.

The ugly duckling was frightened. He flapped his wings and knocked over a milk pail. The farmer's wife chased him out of the house.

Somehow, the ugly duckling found his way to a swamp, and there he managed to live for the rest of the long, hard winter.

When spring came, the ugly duckling found his wings had grown bigger and stronger. He flew across the fields to a canal. There, he saw the beautiful birds he had seen last autumn.

"Hello!" they said.

The ugly duckling looked around. He couldn't believe they were talking to him!

"We are swans," explained one of the birds. "And so are you – you are a very fine young swan indeed!"

The ugly duckling looked down at his reflection in the water. It was true – a handsome swan looked back at him!

The other swans made a circle around him and nuzzled him with their beaks. "Welcome," they said. "We would be happy to have you in our flock!"

The new young swan thought his heart would burst.

"I never dreamed I could be so happy," he thought, "when I was a little ugly duckling."

And, looking around at his new friends, he knew that he would be happy forever.

Hamster Sleepover

Ali looked out of her bedroom window. There, at last, were her best friends coming up the garden path.

Ashley and Martha had sleeping bags under their arms. Daisy was holding a green duvet. They all saw her and waved.

"This is going to be the best sleepover party ever!" Ali said. She jumped off her bed and ran down the stairs two at a time.

After a supper of pizza and chocolate cake – everyone's favourite – the girls got ready for bed.

"Ali has never wanted to go to bed this early before!" joked her mum.

As the four friends snuggled down for the night in Ali's room, there was a loud scratching noise at the bedroom door.

"What's that?" asked Daisy.

They all heard a loud miaow.

"It's Tiger!" said Ali with a grin. Tiger was Ali's cat. "I think she wants to come in and play!"

"Should I let her in?" asked Martha, getting up.

There was a sudden shout from Daisy. "No! Don't open the door!" she said. "Where's Lulu? She isn't in her cage!"

The girls all looked at the hamster cage in the corner of the room. Daisy was right. Ali's hamster, Lulu, was missing.

"Oh no!" said Ali. "We have to find her! Quick!"

The girls began a mad hunt for Lulu, while Tiger scratched at the bedroom door.

"Hang on, Tiger!" Ashley called. "You can't come in yet!"

Daisy searched under Ali's bed. Ashley looked through the pile of sleeping bags. Martha checked behind the bookcase. There was no sign of Lulu.

Ali opened a drawer. "Sometimes she likes to sleep in my socks," she said. But Lulu wasn't there either.

"Where can she be?" Ali groaned.

Just then, Martha spotted something. "Look!" she said.

The girls laughed. They had found Lulu at last, curled up fast asleep in one of Ali's pink slippers.

"She's having her very own sleepover!" Ali said.

Gilly Silly Jarter

Gilly Silly Jarter,
Who has lost a garter,
In a shower of rain,
The miller found it,
The miller ground it,
And the miller gave it
To Silly again.

The Broom Song

Here's a large one for the lady,
Here's a small one for the baby;
Come buy, my pretty lady,
Come buy o' me a broom.

Cock Crow

The cock's on the wood pile
Blowing his horn,
The bull's in the barn
A-threshing the corn.

Chairs to Mend

If I'd as much money as I could spend,
I never would cry, "Old chairs to mend.
Old chairs to mend! Old chairs to mend!"
I never would cry, "Old chairs to mend!"

Puss in the Pantry

Hie, hie, says Anthony,
Puss is in the pantry,
Gnawing, gnawing,
A mutton, mutton bone;
See how she tumbles it,
See how she mumbles it,
See how she tosses
The mutton, mutton bone.

My Maid Mary

My maid Mary,
She minds the dairy,
While I go a-hoeing and mowing each morn;
Merrily runs the reel,
And the little spinning wheel,
Whilst I am singing and mowing my corn.

The Owl and the Pussycat

The Owl and the Pussycat went to sea
In a beautiful pea-green boat.
They took some honey, and plenty of money,
Wrapped up in a five-pound note.
The Owl looked up to the stars above,
And sang to a small guitar,
"O lovely Pussy! O Pussy my love
What a beautiful Pussy you are, you are!
What a beautiful Pussy you are!"

Ten in the Bed

There were ten in the bed and the little one said,
"Roll over! Roll over!"
So they all rolled over and one fell out.

There were nine in the bed and the little one said,
"Roll over! Roll over!"
So they all rolled over and one fell out.

There were eight in the bed and the little one said,
"Roll over! Roll over!"
So they all rolled over and one fell out.

There were seven in the bed and the little one said,
"Roll over! Roll over!"
So they all rolled over and one fell out.

Etc.

The Rainy Day

Rain! It splashed on the windows, gurgled down the drainpipes, and made puddles all over the yard. And Danny and Rosie were bored. Bored, bored, bored!

Out in the pigsty, Bessie and her piglets wallowed in a giant mud bath. It was such fun! There were squeals of delight.

On the pond, the ducks bobbed along looking pleased with themselves. Rain was just water off a duck's back!

Down by the bridge, the river was rising higher and higher. Eventually, it spilled over its banks and brown muddy water flowed across the road and under the farm gate.

Joe was busy fixing the tractor in the barn when he heard a shout from the road and saw Jack the postman struggling through the water on his bike.

"Help, Joe! I'm stranded!" called Jack.

"Don't worry, Jack," Joe shouted back. "We'll get you across."

Joe put down his tools and climbed up into the tractor cab. He started the engine and reversed out of the barn.

Rosie and Danny came out of the house in their waterproofs and ran down to the bridge with Conker the dog.

"Look," gasped Rosie. "The ducklings are swimming all over the garden. And Jack's trapped by the flood!"

Joe rumbled up in the tractor. "Get on the trailer," he shouted to the children. "I'll reverse it through the flood."

"Nice weather for ducks," puffed Jack, as he scrambled aboard. "Thanks, kids. Oh, no! There goes my cap!"

Conker barked wildly and jumped in after it.

"Come back, Conker," cried Rosie. "You'll be swept away!"

"No he won't, silly," said Danny. "Conker's a champion swimmer. Go fetch it, boy!"

Conker grabbed the postman's cap in his mouth, and paddled back to the trailer. He dropped it and wagged his tail.

"Good old Conker!" shouted everyone. "Well done, boy!" Conker shook himself furiously, spraying them all with water.

Joe drove back to the yard and they all jumped off the trailer.

"Thank you, everyone," said Jack, picking up his cap. "Especially you, Conker. I'm very fond of this old cap."

"Come inside," called Mum. "You're all wet through. And what a lot of excitement for a wet Tuesday morning!"

"Brave dog," said Danny, giving Conker a pat.

Spring

Sound the flute!
Now it's mute!
Birds delight,
Day and night,
Nightingale,
In the dale,
Lark in sky,
Merrily,
Merrily merrily, to welcome in the year.

Little boy,
Full of joy;
Little girl,
Sweet and small;
Cock does crow,
So do you;
Merry voice,
Infant noise;
Merrily, merrily, to welcome in the year.

All the Bells Were Ringing

All the bells were ringing
And all the birds were singing,
When Molly sat down crying
For her broken doll:
Oh you silly Moll!
Sobbing and sighing
For a broken doll,
When all the bells are ringing
And all the birds are singing.

The Gossips

Miss One, Two, and Three
Could never agree,
While they gossiped around
A tea-caddy.

Engine, Engine

Engine, engine, number nine,
Sliding down Chicago line;
When she's polished she will shine,
Engine, engine, number nine.

Buff

I had a dog
Whose name was Buff,
I sent him for
A bag of snuff;
He broke the bag
And spilt the stuff,
And that was all
My penny's worth.

Puss at the Door

Who's that ringing at my doorbell?
A little pussycat that isn't very well.
Rub its little nose with a little mutton fat,
That's the best cure for a little pussycat.

Three Ghostesses

Three little ghostesses,
Sitting on postesses,
Eating buttered toastesses,
Greasing their fistesses,
Up to their wristesses.
Oh what beastesses
To make such feastesses!

Washing Day

The old woman must stand
At the tub, tub, tub,
The dirty clothes to rub, rub, rub;
But when they are clean,
And fit to be seen,
She'll dress like a lady
And dance on the green.

The Ant and the Grasshopper

Grasshopper was a lively, happy insect, who didn't have a care in the world. He spent the long summer days relaxing in the sunshine or bouncing and dancing through the grass.

"Why are you working so hard?" asked Grasshopper one day, when he saw Ant struggling to carry some grain on her back. "It's such a sunny day! Come and play!"

"I've got no time, Grasshopper," said Ant. "I have to take this grain back to my nest, so that my family and I have enough food when winter comes. Have you built your nest yet?"

"Nest?" laughed Grasshopper. "Who needs a nest when life in the great outdoors is so wonderful? And there's plenty of food – why should I worry?"

Day after day, Grasshopper played, while Ant worked. Soon the trees began to lose their leaves and the days began to get shorter and cooler. But lazy Grasshopper hardly noticed. He was still too busy enjoying himself.

A few days later, it began to snow. Grasshopper suddenly found himself cold and all alone. He was hungry and there wasn't a crumb of food to be found anywhere!

"I know," said Grasshopper. "Ant will help me." So he set out to look for Ant's nest. It was safe and warm beneath a rock.

Ant came out to see him. "What do you want?" she asked.

"Please, Ant," said Grasshopper, "have you any food to spare?"

Ant looked at him. "All summer long, while we worked hard to gather food and prepare our nest, what did you do?"

"I played and had fun, of course," said Grasshopper. "That's what summer is for!"

"Well, you were wrong, weren't you," said Ant. "If you play all summer, then you must go hungry all winter."

"Yes," said Grasshopper sadly, as a tiny tear fell from the corner of his eye. "I've learned my lesson now. I just hope it isn't too late!"

Ant's heart softened. "Alright, come on in," she said. "I'll find some food for you."

Grasshopper gratefully crawled into the warm nest, where Ant and her family shared their food with him.

By the time spring came around, Grasshopper was fat and fit and ready to start building a nest of his very own!

Aunty and the Flowers

Every year on the farm, the animals had a competition. Everyone liked to join in the fun, and there was a prize for the winner. The prize could be for anything. One year, it was for growing the best purple vegetables.

This year the prize was for the best display of flowers, and it was Aunty the goat's turn to judge the prize.

On the day of the competition, Aunty came into the tent first. She looked very important as she was taken to the first display made by Bramble the sheep.

"So I just choose which flowers I like best?" Aunty asked.

"Yes, we walk along the table, and whichever display you think is best wins the prize. This is Bramble's display. He's spent all morning getting it right," said Blink the pig.

"It's called 'Daisies and Dandelions'," said Bramble proudly.

The flowers were white and yellow and looked very pretty in a blue mug. Aunty looked at them carefully. She sniffed them. And then she ate them.

The others were so surprised that they couldn't speak!

They just stared as Aunty went to the next display, 'Buttercups and Roses'. She ate them too!

The goat tilted her head back, half-closed her eyes in a very thoughtful sort of way, and compared 'Buttercups and Roses' with 'Daisies and Dandelions'.

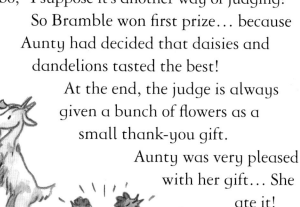

Moving along the line, she ate 'Cowslips and Honeysuckle'. Then she ate 'Chrysanthemums and Poppies'.

Aunty wrinkled up her nose. "Bit sour, that," she said. She turned at last and saw all the others looking at her with their mouths open.

"What?" she said, puzzled.

"What?" Rambo the bull said. "You were supposed to judge how pretty the flowers are!"

"Flowers are pretty as well as tasty?" asked Aunty.

Everyone burst out laughing.

"Well," said Rambo, "I suppose it's another way of judging!"

So Bramble won first prize... because Aunty had decided that daisies and dandelions tasted the best!

At the end, the judge is always given a bunch of flowers as a small thank-you gift.

Aunty was very pleased with her gift... She ate it!

Hazel Squirrel

Hazel Squirrel had the finest tail of all the animals that lived beside Looking-Glass Pond.

It was fluffier than Dilly Duck's tail... bushier than Harvey Rabbit's tail... and swooshier than everybody's!

Each morning Hazel groomed her tail and admired her reflection in the pond. "I really do have a beautiful tail!" she would say, smiling at herself in the silvery water.

Sometimes Hazel played with her friends, but it usually ended in tears.

"You splashed my lovely tail!" Hazel would shout crossly, when she played leap-frog with Webster.

"You're getting my tail dirty, Harvey!" she would moan

very grumpily, when they played digging.

Soon, Hazel stopped playing with her friends altogether. "I'm far too busy brushing my tail!" she said whenever they came to call. "Come back some other time."

One morning, Hazel was admiring her tail by the pond as usual. Suddenly, she had a funny thought. She couldn't remember the last time she had seen her friends.

Hazel looked at her reflection in the pond. Staring back was a strange face… a cross face… a grumpy face. It was Hazel's face! Hazel couldn't believe her eyes. "No wonder my friends don't visit any more," she cried. "I've forgotten how to smile!"

The next day Hazel called for her friends. They had such fun playing leap-frog and digging muddy holes that she forgot all about her tail. "From now on," she laughed, "the only time I'll look at my reflection is to practise smiling!"

The Dragon Who Was Scared of Flying

Once upon a time, in a land far away, there lived a dragon named Dennis who was scared of flying.

Every day his friends would set off to have adventures, leaving poor Dennis behind on his own. And every evening, the other dragons would return to their caves on the mountain with amazing tales of what they had been up to that day.

"I rescued a damsel in distress," one would say.

"I fought the evil one-eyed giant and won," boasted another.

One day, Dennis could stand it no longer. Instead of retreating into his cave, he set off down the mountainside. It was very tiring having to walk. Dennis was about to have a rest when he saw some brightly coloured tents in the distance.

"I might take a closer look," thought Dennis. "Maybe I can have an adventure, too!"

When Dennis reached the tents he found himself in a world more exotic than he could ever have imagined. There were acrobats and tightrope walkers and trapeze artists, horses and clowns and a very fat ringmaster in a red coat. In such an incredible place no one gave Dennis a second look. They just assumed he was part of the show!

The only person who knew for sure that Dennis wasn't part of the circus was Claude the ringmaster – because he owned it!

"Hello, there!" he said. "Welcome to Claude's Circus. How do you do?"

"I'm Dennis the dragon," said Dennis.

"A dragon, eh?" said Claude. "Might be quite a crowd-puller! Would you like to join us?"

So Dennis joined the circus. Soon he was the circus's champion fire-eater. Folk would come from far and near to see Dennis shooting flames high into the dark roof of the big top.

One evening, when Dennis had finished his act, he sat watching Carlotta, the tightrope walker, pirouetting high up on the rope as usual. All at once she lost her footing. Dennis saw to his horror that she was going to fall. Without thinking, he flapped his wings furiously – and found himself flying up towards her. He caught her and flew down to the ground. The crowd burst into applause. They obviously thought it was all part of the act.

"Thank you, Dennis," whispered Carlotta. "You saved my life."

Dennis was overjoyed. Not only had he saved Carlotta's life, he had also learned to fly. And, he said with a grin, "I do declare that flying is actually rather fun."

Thank You

Thank you for your portrait,
I think it's very nice.
I've put it in the attic
To scare away the mice.

Cock Robin's Courtship

Cock Robin got up early
At the break of day,
And went to Jenny's window
To sing a roundelay.
He sang Cock Robin's love
To little Jenny Wren,
And when he got unto the end
Then he began again.

Grig's Pig

Grandpa Grig
Had a pig,
In a field of clover;
Piggy died,
Grandpa cried,
And all the fun was over.

Little Betty Blue

Little Betty Blue
Lost a holiday shoe,
What can little Betty do?
Give her another
To match the other,
And then she may
Swagger in two.

See-saw, Margery Daw

See-saw, Margery Daw,
Johnny shall have a new master;
He shall have but a penny a day,
Because he can't work any faster.

Elsie Marley

Elsie Marley's grown so fine,
She won't get up to feed the swine,
But lies in bed till eight or nine,
Lazy Elsie Marley!

The Swing

How do you like to go up in a swing,
Up in the air so blue?
Oh, I do think it the pleasantest thing
Ever a child can do!

Up in the air and over the wall,
Till I can see so wide,
River and trees and cattle and all
Over the countryside –

Till I look down on the garden green,
Down on the roof so brown –
Up in the air I go flying again,
Up in the air and down!

City Child

Dainty little maiden, whither would you wander?
Whither from this pretty home, the home where mother dwells?
"Far and far away," said the dainty little maiden,
"All among the gardens, auriculas, anemones,
Roses and lilies and Canterbury-bells."

Dainty little maiden, whither would you wander?
Whither from this pretty house, this city house of ours?
"Far and far away," said the dainty little maiden,
"All among the meadows, the clover and the clematis,
Daisies and kingcups and honeysuckle-flowers."

Copycat Max

Max was a little tiger with a bad habit. He copied everyone! When the parrot said, "Pretty Polly," Max repeated it. Then, when the parrot got cross and said, "Shut up, Max," he repeated that as well. It was very annoying.

One day, Max set off to annoy as many animals as possible.

Soon he met a brown chameleon sitting on a green leaf. The chameleon saw Max and changed his colour to green.

"Watch this then," said Max, and he rolled over and over in some mud. "Now I'm brown," he said.

"You're not really brown," said the chameleon. "Only chameleons can change colour."

"Hmmm!" said Max, annoyed. He rolled in some white feathers. They stuck to the mud. "Look," he said, "now I'm white!"

The chameleon started to laugh. "It won't last," he said.

When Max got home his mother was very angry with him for getting so dirty. She held Max down with her big paw and licked him until he was clean again. It took *ages*. Max wriggled and complained but he couldn't get away.

"It serves you right for being such a copycat," said his mother. "I hope you've learnt your lesson not to do it again."

"Oh, all right," said Max. And, for the moment, he meant it!

Forever Friends

Daisy Duckling had lots of friends but her best friend of all was Cilla Cygnet. Every day they played together, chasing each other through the reeds.

"When I grow up, I'll be a beautiful swan like my mummy!" said Cilla.

"And I'll be a dull brown duck," said Daisy. She worried that Cilla would only want to play with her pretty swan friends when they grew up.

One day, the two were playing hide-and-seek when something dreadful happened. While Daisy hid amongst some large dock leaves, a sly fox crept up and snatched her in his mouth!

Before she had time to quack he was heading for his lair. But Cilla had been watching. Without hesitating she rushed after the fox and caught the tip of his long tail in her sharp beak. Then, as the fox spun round, she pecked him hard on the nose.

The fox's mouth dropped open and Daisy fell out. He slunk away.

Daisy couldn't thank Cilla enough.

"That's what friends are for!" said Cilla. "We'll always be friends."

And Mrs Swan and Mrs Duck, who were the best of friends, couldn't agree more.

My Grandad Is Great

My grandad is great. He always has lots of time for me, even when he's busy.

I always look forward to going to stay with him for the weekend. Grandad is a lot like me. He enjoys getting lovely and dirty. (I just wish Grandma felt the same way.)

My grandad is a great fisherman, but he always forgets the size of the fish that he caught.

Luckily, I'm there to remind him!

Grandad is a brilliant gardener. His pumpkins are the biggest I've ever seen.

(Well, that was until I saw some even bigger ones at the village show.)

Grandad knows all about the countryside. He knows the names of every bird and flower.

Grandad is a fantastic dancer.

I love dancing with him, but sometimes it makes me feel a bit dizzy. I don't know where he gets his energy.

Grandad is very handy in the house. I can't wait to show Grandma the railway set he's built in the kitchen! And he's a brilliant cook, too. He says that when I grow up he'll tell me the secret of making a really good pizza.

Grandad tells me all kinds of amazing stories. It's hard to believe that he used to be a pirate! I wish I could have seen his big, red pirate ship.

Sometimes, if I'm really lucky, Grandad lets me sleep in his tent. When he's with me, I'm never afraid.

When it's time to go home, I wave goodbye to Grandad. I expect he's really busy when I'm not there to help him out with everything.

I love going to Grandad's because... my grandad is *great*!

Snow White

One day, a queen gave birth to a beautiful little girl, who had skin as white as snow, cheeks as red as blood, and hair as black as ebony wood. She was called Snow White.

Sadly, the queen soon died. The king married again, and the new queen was beautiful but vain. Every day she stood before her magic mirror and asked: "Mirror, mirror, on the wall, who is the fairest one of all?"

The mirror always said: "You, oh Queen, are fairest of all!"

But little Snow White grew more and more lovely. At last the day came when the queen's magic mirror replied: "You, oh Queen, are fair, it's true. But Snow White is fairer than you!"

The queen was very angry. She summoned her huntsman.

"Take Snow White into the forest and kill her," said the wicked queen. "Bring me her heart in this chest."

So the huntsman took Snow White deep into the forest. But when he looked at Snow White he could not do it.

The huntsman killed a wild pig, put its heart in the chest and returned to the castle. The wicked queen was pleased, for she was sure that Snow White was dead.

Lost and alone, Snow White
stumbled through the dark forest
until she came to a little cottage.
She knocked at the door, but there
was no answer. The door was
unlocked, so she walked in.

Inside, she saw a little table with
seven little plates of food. Snow
White was hungry and ate some of the food.

Soon, Snow White felt sleepy. She found seven cosy little
beds. She lay down on one of them and fell fast asleep.

The cottage belonged to seven dwarfs who worked in the
gold mines. When they returned home that night, they found
Snow White. She told them her story. They felt sorry for her.

"If you cook and clean for us," they said, "you can stay here
and we will look after you." So Snow White decided to stay.

At the castle, the wicked queen was looking in her magic
mirror. This time the mirror said: "Snow White is as lovely as
she is good. She lives with the dwarfs, deep in the wood!"

The queen was furious. She decided to kill Snow White
herself. She made a magic potion and used it to poison a pretty
hair comb. Then she set out for the dwarfs' cottage dressed as a
poor peasant woman.

"Pretty combs to buy!" she cried.

Snow White went outside. The witch offered to comb Snow
White's hair. When the poisoned comb touched Snow White's
beautiful black hair, she fell to the floor as if she were dead.

That night when the dwarfs came home, they found Snow White lying in the cottage garden.

At first they were in despair, but then one of them noticed the comb. Very gently, the eldest dwarf took the comb out of Snow White's hair. Soon, her pale cheeks grew rosy again.

The next morning, when the dwarfs left for the mines, they made sure Snow White locked the door and they kept the key.

This time, when the queen's magic mirror told her that Snow White was still alive, she roared with fury.

The wicked queen made a magic potion. With the potion she poisoned one half of a rosy apple. Then she set off to the dwarfs' cottage dressed as an apple-seller.

"Sweet, rosy apples to buy!" she called outside the window. But Snow White remembered the dwarfs' warning.

"I cannot let you in and I cannot come out," she said.

"Where is the harm in a sweet, rosy apple?" asked the apple-seller. "Look, I will take a bite from this side. It is so sweet and juicy! Taste it for yourself."

Snow White took the poisoned apple. The moment she bit the poisoned apple, she fell down, lifeless.

When the dwarfs found Snow White lying on the floor again, they did everything they could to try to wake her. But she was still and cold.

The dwarfs made a beautiful glass coffin for Snow White. They set it among the flowers in their garden.

One day, a prince came riding through the forest. When he saw Snow White, he instantly fell in love with her. He begged the dwarfs to let him take the casket to his palace.

When the dwarfs lifted the casket, they stumbled. Suddenly a piece of poisoned apple fell from Snow White's mouth and her eyes opened. Snow White was alive!

Of course, the moment Snow White set eyes on the prince, she fell in love with him. When he asked Snow White to marry him, she happily agreed.

The next time the wicked queen looked into her magic mirror, it said: "You, oh Queen, are fair, it is true. But there is one still fairer than you. The bride that the prince will marry tonight is none other than the lovely Snow White!"

The wicked queen was so enraged that she fell down dead. And Snow White had nothing to fear ever again.

Mary, Mary, Quite Contrary

Mary, Mary, quite contrary,
How does your garden grow?
With silver bells and cockle shells,
And pretty maids all in a row.

A Farthing

I went into my grandmother's garden,
And there I found a farthing.
I went into my next door neighbour's;
There I bought
A pipkin and a popkin,
A slipkin and a slopkin,
A nailboard, a sailboard,
And all for a farthing.

Here Comes a Widow

Here comes a widow from Barbary-land,
With all her children in her hand;
One can brew, and one can bake,
And one can make a wedding-cake.
Pray take one, pray take two,
Pray take one that pleases you.

Jack Sprat's Cat

Jack Sprat
Had a cat,
It had but one ear;
It went to buy butter
When butter was dear.

Butterfly

I'm a little butterfly
Born in a bower,
Christened in a teapot,
Died in half an hour.

An Egg

In marble halls as white as milk,
Lined with skin as soft as silk;
Within a fountain crystal clear,
A golden apple doth appear.
No doors there are to this stronghold –
Yet thieves break in and steal the gold.

Grumpy Fairy

Misery didn't have any friends. It was her own fault, she was always grumbling. Willow, her niece, couldn't understand

her. "Why do you always find fault with everyone?" she asked.

"Because everybody is so useless!" said her grumpy aunt.

One day Misery told the fairy who baked the bread, "Your bread is too soft. I like crusty bread."

"If that's your attitude," said the baker fairy, "bake your own bread!"

"I shall!" said Misery.

The next day she was rude to the fairy who mended her shoes.

"No one speaks to me like that!" said the cobbler fairy. "From now on you can mend your own shoes."

"I'll be glad to," said Misery grumpily.

Then she insulted the fairy who collected honey from the bees.

"How dare you?" said the honey-collector fairy. "I'm not staying here to be insulted. You can collect your own honey."

"How are you going to manage?" Willow asked Misery.

"No problem," said Misery. "I'll do everything myself." And with that she set to work to bake some bread. Misery mixed and kneaded the dough and left it to rise. Then she put the loaf in the oven, and sat down for a well-earned rest. Soon she had nodded off.

She was woken by a smell of burning. All that was left of the loaf of bread were a few burnt cinders. What Misery didn't realize was that the baker fairy used a special baking spell – a spell that Misery didn't know!

Misery went to collect some honey. She waved her arms at the bees buzzing round the hive, shouting, "Out of my way, bees." They didn't like it one little bit! Their answer was to swarm around her and sting her. You see, what Misery didn't know was that the honey fairy used a special honey-collecting spell.

Misery ran from the bees as fast as she could. As she did, she broke her shoe! Oh dear! What a state she was in! Burnt bread, bee stings and only one shoe!

"You can't go on like this," said Willow, when she saw Misery.

Misery did some serious thinking. "Tell all the fairies I've turned over a new leaf," she told Willow. "From now on I shan't be grumpy any more."

Willow was delighted! Misery didn't complain about anything for months after that, and Willow kept her fingers crossed that it would last.

The Little Doll

I once had a sweet little doll, dears,
The prettiest doll in the world;
Her cheeks were so red and white, dears,
And her hair was so charmingly curled.
But I lost my poor little doll, dears,
As I played in the heath one day;
And I cried for her more than a week, dears,
But I never could find where she lay.

I found my poor little doll, dears,
As I played in the heath one day;
Folks say she is terribly changed, dears,
For her paint is all washed away,
And her arms trodden off by the cows, dears,
And her hair not the least bit curled;
Yet for old sakes' sake, she is still, dears,
The prettiest doll in the world.

Skipping

Little children skip,
The rope so gaily gripping,
Tom and Harry,
Jane and Mary,
Kate, Diana,
Susan, Anna,
All are fond of skipping!

The little boats they skip,
Beside the heavy shipping,
And while the squalling
Winds are calling,
Falling, rising,
Rising, falling,
All are fond of skipping!

The autumn leaves they skip,
When blasts the trees are stripping;
Bounding, whirling,
Sweeping, twirling,
And in wanton
Mazes curling,
All are fond of skipping!

Lion's Birthday

It was Lion's birthday.

"Hello, Elephant! Hello, Parrot!" said Lion.

"Er, hello!" trumpeted Elephant. They were both carrying bunches of flowers. "Sorry, Lion. We're kind of busy right now."

"Hello, Giraffe! Hello, Monkey!" said Lion. They were collecting coconuts from a tall palm tree.

"We're too busy to talk!" said Giraffe over his shoulder.

"Hello, Zebra! Hello, Hippo!" said Lion.

Zebra muttered something to Hippo. They disappeared behind a pineapple tree without even saying hello!

"The animals have all forgotten my birthday," said Lion, sadly. He walked slowly through the jungle, feeling very sad.

Then... "*Happy birthday, Lion!*" called all the animals.

"What a *surprise!*" roared Lion happily.

Sad Monkey

Tiny Monkey was sad because he didn't know how to climb.

"All the other monkeys can climb," he thought.

"I'll teach you, Tiny Monkey," said Big Monkey, scampering up a tree. "Cling with your feet, and swing your tail – like this!"

"I'll lift you up into the tree to get you going," said Giraffe.

"I'll catch you if you fall down," said Lion.

"See if you can get all the way up to the top!" said Parrot, fluttering up to the topmost branch in a flash of colour and then flying back down again.

Taking a deep breath, Tiny Monkey climbed onto Giraffe's neck. Her neck swayed as she lifted him high into the tree. Tiny Monkey took a deep breath and swung into the tree.

He clung with his feet and swung with his tail, just as Big Monkey had told him. And it worked! He scampered all the way to the top!

"Look at me! I'm the best climbing monkey in the forest!" he called.

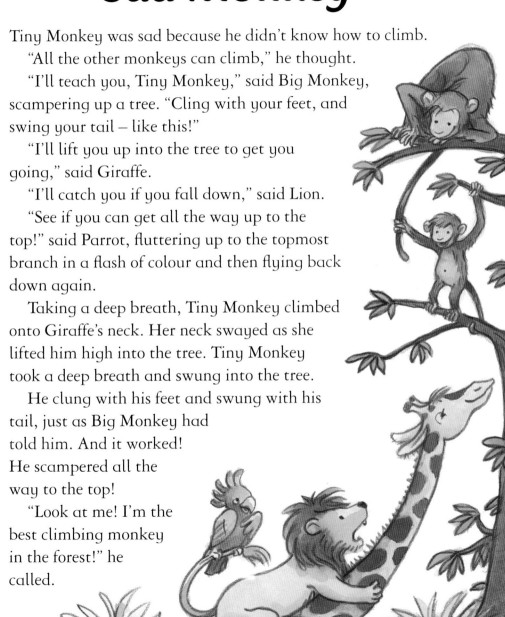

Surprise Sleepover

It had been snowing all day. Ali, Daisy and Martha were at Ashley's house. Though it was still afternoon, it was growing dark already.

Suddenly the light in Ashley's room went out, and everything went very, very dark.

"What's happening?" yelled Ali. The girls grabbed each other's hands in the dark.

"Let's go downstairs," said Ashley.

They stumbled forwards and Ashley felt for the door handle. Finding it, she pulled the door open and the others followed her out onto the landing.

The light had gone out there too. It was as black as night.

Ashley's mum came up the stairs holding a candle. "Don't panic, girls, it's just a power cut!" she said. "Come on,

we'll make ourselves cosy in the sitting room."

Downstairs, Ashley's dad was building a fire in the hearth. "The snow's knocked out the power," he said. "And the roads are all blocked."

"But how will we get home?" Ali asked.

Ashley's mum told them not to worry and went to ring their parents.

Ashley's dad went to fetch some duvets. "Here, girls," he said. "These will keep you warm until the fire gets going."

The girls snuggled up on the two sofas and watched as the fire began to crackle to life.

Ashley's mum came in a little later with some drinks. "I've got a bit of a surprise, girls!" she said. "Guess what?"

"What, Mum?" asked Ashley.

"You're all going to stay here tonight because of the snow!" she said with a smile. "You're having a surprise sleepover!"

"Yay!" they all cheered.

"Snowstorms are great!" said Martha.

Minnie and Mattie

Minnie and Mattie
And fat little May,
Out in the country,
Spending a day.

Minnie and Mattie
And May carry posies,
Half of sweet violets,
Half of primroses.

Give the sun time enough,
Glowing and glowing,
He'll rouse the roses
And bring them blowing.

Don't wait for roses,
Losing today,
Oh Minnie, Mattie,
And wise little May.

Violets and primroses
Blossom today,
For Minnie and Mattie
And fat little May.

Meg Merrilees

Old Meg she was a gypsy,
And lived upon the moors:
Her bed it was the brown heath turf,
And her house was out of doors.

Her brothers were the craggy hills,
Her sisters larchen trees –
Alone with her great family
She lived as she did please.

No breakfast had she many a morn,
No dinner many a noon,
And 'stead of supper she would stare
Full hard against the moon.

Old Meg was brave as Margaret Queen,
And tall as Amazon:
An old red blanket cloak she wore;
A chip-hat had she on.
God rest her aged bones somewhere –
She died full long agone!

There Was an Old Woman Who Lived in a Shoe

There was an old woman who lived in a shoe,
She had so many children she didn't know what to do;
She gave them some broth without any bread,
Then scolded them soundly and put them to bed.

There Was an Old Woman Tossed Up in a Basket

There was an old woman tossed up in a basket,
Nineteen times as high as the moon;
Where she was going I couldn't but ask it,
For in her hand she carried a broom.

"Old woman, old woman, old woman," quoth I,
"Oh whither, Oh whither, Oh whither so high?"
"To brush the cobwebs off the sky!"
"Shall I go with thee?" "Aye, by and by."

My Grandma Is Great

My grandma is great.

She's gentle, kind and lots of fun. Sometimes when Mum and Dad go out for the evening, I go to Grandma's house to sleep. I always have a fantastic time because my grandma makes me feel special.

Grandma always knows exactly what I like to eat. She gives me the yummiest food.

(That's our little secret – don't tell Mum and Dad!)

My grandma likes me to help her around the house. She calls me her "little helper".

I don't know how she manages when I'm not here.

Grandma never gets cross, even when I make a terrible mess. And she always likes my cooking.

I can't wait for her to taste my rock cakes.

Grandma doesn't mind how noisy I am. She even bought me a brilliant set of drums.

Won't Mum and Dad be pleased?

My grandma has lots of interesting hobbies. She's the coolest grandma I know.

And she knits me fabulous jumpers.

(Well... my toy giraffe likes the jumpers, anyway.)

My grandma loves playing games. She likes lots of games, but her favourite game of all is hide-and-seek.

I normally hide and she looks for me.

I'm so good at hiding that she never finds me. Or at least she pretends she can't find me, even when I think she knows where I am.

At bedtime, Grandma tells me funny stories about Dad when he was a little boy. She says that he was quite naughty.

I don't believe that Dad was ever naughty, but the stories make me laugh anyway. She makes me laugh so much that I get hiccups.

But my grandma's so great that she knows exactly how to get rid of them.

I'm always sad when I kiss Grandma goodbye. But she only lives next door, so I pop over to see her whenever I want because... my grandma is *great!*

Lucy Locket

Lucy Locket lost her pocket,
Kitty Fisher found it.
Not a penny was there in it,
Only ribbon round it.

Ice Cream

Ice cream, ice cream, a penny a lump!
The more you eat, the more you jump.

If Pigs Could Fly

If pigs could fly
High in the sky,
Where do you think they'd go?
Would they follow a plane
To France or Spain,
Or drift where the wind blows?

The Wind

When the wind is in the East,
'Tis neither good to man nor beast.
When the wind is in the North,
The skilful fisher goes not forth.
When the wind is in the South,
It blows the bait in the fish's mouth.
When the wind is in the West,
Then it is at its very best.

Kindness

If I had a donkey that would not go,
Would I beat him? Oh no, no.
I'd put him in the barn and give him some corn,
The best little donkey that ever was born.

Little Friend

In the greenhouse lives a wren,
Little friend of little men;
When they're good she tells them where
To find the apple, quince and pear.

Cinderella

Once upon a time there was a pretty young girl who lived with her father, stepmother and two stepsisters. The stepmother was unkind, and the stepsisters were mean.

Every day, the girl got up at dawn to cook and clean and wash and sew for her stepmother and stepsisters. Every night, the stepmother told the girl to sleep beside the fire. Soon the girl's clothes and hair were so grey with ash and cinders that everyone called her Cinderella.

One morning, a special invitation arrived. All the young women in the kingdom were invited to a ball at the royal palace so that the young prince could choose a bride.

The two stepsisters were very excited and ordered Cinderella around as she helped them get ready for the ball.

Cinderella sighed. She wished she could go with them.

As an elegant carriage took her stepsisters to the ball, Cinderella sat beside the hearth and wept.

"I wish I could go to the ball," she cried.

Suddenly, a strange light filled the room.

Cinderella looked up. A silvery glow surrounded a kind-looking woman with a glittering wand.

"Who are you?" asked Cinderella, blinking in wonder.

"I am your fairy godmother," she replied. "I have come to help you go to the ball."

"But how?" asked Cinderella.

"Find me a big pumpkin, six white mice, six frogs and a rat," said the fairy godmother.

Cinderella found everything as quickly as she could.

The fairy godmother tapped the pumpkin with her wand. The pumpkin changed into a magnificent golden coach.

Next, the fairy godmother waved her wand over the six white mice. The six mice became six prancing horses.

The fairy godmother gently tapped her wand and the six frogs changed into handsome footmen. One more tap, and the rat became a smart coachman.

With one last gentle tap of the wand, Cinderella's dusty dress became a shimmering ball gown. On her feet were two sparkling glass slippers.

"Now," said the fairy godmother, "you are ready for the ball. But at the stroke of midnight the magic will end, and everything will change back to what it was."

Cinderella promised to be home before midnight.

When Cinderella arrived at the palace, everyone turned to look at her. No one knew who Cinderella was. Even her own stepsisters didn't recognize her.

The prince thought that she was the loveliest, most enchanting girl he had ever seen. He danced only with her.

As Cinderella whirled round the room in his arms, she felt so happy that she forgot her fairy godmother's warning.

Suddenly, she heard the clock chime… twelve times!

"I must go!" cried Cinderella. And before the prince could stop her, she ran from the ballroom and out of the palace.

"Wait!" cried the prince, dashing after her. But by the time he reached the palace steps, all he could see was a ragged kitchen maid hurrying towards the palace gates.

Then he saw something twinkling on the steps – a single glass slipper. The prince picked it up.

"I will marry the woman whose foot fits this glass slipper," he declared. "I will search the kingdom until I find her."

The next day, the prince began going from house to house, looking for his true love. Every young woman in the kingdom tried on the glass slipper, but it didn't fit anyone.

At last the prince came to Cinderella's house. Her stepsisters were waiting to try on the slipper.

The first stepsister pushed and squeezed, but she could barely get her fat toes into the tiny slipper.

The second stepsister also tried to cram her foot into the shoe. But it was no use.

The prince was turning to leave when a soft voice asked, "May I try the slipper, please?"

As Cinderella stepped forward to try on the slipper, her stepsisters began to laugh.

"Get back to the kitchen where you belong!" ordered her stepmother.

"Everyone should have a chance," said the prince, "even a kitchen maid."

Cinderella sat down and took off her rough wooden clogs. The prince held out the sparkling slipper. And suddenly...

"Oh!" gasped her stepsisters.

Of course, Cinderella's dainty foot fitted into the slipper perfectly.

As her stepsisters gazed in amazement, the prince joyfully took Cinderella in his arms.

Her stepsisters and stepmother were still trembling with shock as they watched Cinderella ride off to the palace in the prince's own carriage.

Cinderella and the prince were soon married, and lived happily ever after.

Bunny Helps Mummy

It was a good day to dry some washing. The sun was shining and the wind was blowing.

Bunny was helping his mummy by hanging out the washing on the line.

Suddenly the wind blew extra-hard, and it whisked some of the washing away.

"Come back!" cried Bunny, and he chased the washing as it flipped and flapped off through the woods.

He found two noisy birds squabbling over his stripy socks. They wanted to take the socks to line their nests with and make them all cosy for the baby birds.

"I'll have those back, thank you!" cried Bunny.

Then Bunny saw something moving along the ground.

It was brightly coloured. It looked like Daddy's woolly hat, but it was moving!

Bunny cautiously lifted the hat up. Some furry mice peeped out from underneath. They were taking it off to make a soft bed with.

"I'll have that back, thank you!" cried Bunny.

Then Bunny noticed the corner of his baby brother's special blanket poking out from a hole in a tree.

He pulled as hard as he could until out popped the blanket, and out popped a family of furry squirrels. They had been using the blanket to snuggle up in.

"I'll have that back, thank you!" cried Bunny.

Bunny gathered up all the washing in the wood, until he had a big wobbly pile.

He took it all home and he hung it back on the line. It was hard work for a little bunny like him.

When Mummy came outside, all the washing was dry. And Bunny was curled up in the washing basket... fast asleep!

Pyjama Party Disco

It was the school holidays. Ali, Martha and Ashley were at Daisy's for a sleepover.

"Let's have a disco!" said Daisy as they munched on some crisps. "We can use my new disco ball lamp."

"Great idea!" said the others.

Daisy got out her best music for dancing to, and the others looked through Daisy's wardrobe for party clothes to wear.

Once they had all changed, the girls cleared a space on Daisy's bedroom floor and closed the curtains. Daisy put on the music and Ashley switched on the disco ball lamp.

The girls started to sing and dance. Daisy picked up her hairbrush and jumped onto her bed. "Look at me!" she laughed. "I could be a popstar!" Her friends cheered as she sang along, pretending the hairbrush was a microphone.

Before long, Ashley, Ali and Martha were singing and dancing on the bed too.

Just as Ali was in the middle of a high kick there was a loud cracking noise and Daisy's bed collapsed.

Martha and Ashley landed on the floor in a heap, and Ali tripped forwards and crashed into Daisy.

Daisy's big brother Jon came rushing into the room. "What's going on in here?" he grinned. "Disco dancing accident?"

"It's not funny!" said Daisy. "We've broken the bed!"

"I could mend it," said Jon. "I might not even tell Mum. What's it worth?"

The girls looked at each other. "How about half a bar of chocolate?" said Martha.

Jon laughed. "No way! You'll have to do better than that!"

In the end the girls had to promise Jon *all* their sweets and crisps before he went to get the toolbox.

When Jon had fixed the bed the girls got into their pyjamas.

"The next time I'm disco dancing, it's going to be on a proper dance floor!" groaned Daisy.

"Or on stage in front of a huge audience!" laughed Ashley.

The Fairies

Up the airy mountain,
Down the rushy glen,
We daren't go a-hunting
For fear of little men;
Wee folk, good folk,
Trooping all together;
Green jacket, red cap,
And a white owl's feather!

Down along the rocky shore
Some make their home,
They live on crispy pancakes
Of yellow tide-foam;
Some in the reeds
Of the black mountain lake,
With frogs for their watch-dogs,
All night awake.

By the craggy hill-side,
Through the mosses bare,
They have planted thorn-trees
For pleasure here and there.
If any man so daring
As dig them up in spite,
He shall find their sharpest thorns
In his bed at night.

The Butterfly's Ball

Come take up your hats, and away let us haste
To the butterfly's ball, and the grasshopper's feast.
The trumpeter gadfly has summoned the crew,
And the revels are now only waiting for you.

On the smooth-shaven grass by the side of a wood,
Beneath a broad oak that for ages has stood,
See the children of earth, and the tenants of air,
For an evening's amusement together repair.

And there came the moth, with his plumage of down,
And the hornet in jacket of yellow and brown;
Who with him the wasp, his companion, did bring,
But they promised, that evening, to lay by their sting.

With step so majestic the snail did advance,
And promised the gazers a minuet to dance.
But they all laughed so loud that he pull'd in his head,
And went in his own little chamber to bed.

Then, as evening gave way to the shadows of night,
Their watchman, the glow-worm, came out with a light.
Then home let us hasten, while yet we can see,
For no watchman is waiting for you and for me.

Just as Well, Really!

Rumpus liked water. He liked the drippiness and droppiness, the splashiness and sloppiness of it!

He liked it so much that, whenever there was water around, Rumpus somehow always managed to fall into it!

But Mum loved Rumpus, so she simply sighed and she mopped up the mess.

Rumpus loved mud. He loved the way you could plodge in it, splodge in it, slide in it and glide in it!

Rumpus somehow always managed to get covered in it!

But Dad loved Rumpus, so every time he simply sighed and he sponged off the splatters.

Rumpus enjoyed paint. He liked to splatter and dash it, to spread and splash it! Rumpus somehow managed to get it everywhere!

But Rumpus' big brother loved him, so every time he simply sighed and cleaned him up.

Rumpus loved his mum, dad and big brother.

And Rumpus' mum, dad and big brother loved Rumpus… which was just as well, really!

Clara Cow's Cold

One morning, Clara Cow woke up with a tickle in her nose.

"*Aaaa-tishoo!* Oh dear," said Clara. "I think I've caught a nasty cold."

"You should borrow the scarecrow's hat," squeaked the mice. And off they scurried to fetch it.

"*Aaaa-tishoo!* Thank you!" sneezed Clara, even louder, as she put it on.

"You must keep warm," clucked Harriet the hen. "Why don't you borrow that scarf on the washing line?"

"*Aaaa-tishoo!* Good idea!" sneezed Clara, wrapping it round her neck.

Then she sneezed loudly again.

Her loud sneeze woke Danny the duck. "If you've got a cold, you need wellies to keep your feet dry!" he quacked.

"*Aaaa-tishoo!* That might do the trick!" agreed Clara. "I'll borrow the farmer's boots." And she slipped them on.

But Clara just kept on sneezing. "*Aaaa-tishoo!*"

"Time for bed!" ordered her friends, and Clara agreed.

"*Aaaaa....*" began Clara, as she snuggled down. But no sneeze came, just a *big* yawn.

And when Clara woke the next morning her cold was gone!

Utterly Mad

Did you ever see a piglet all dressed up in polka dots,
Or a princess on her wedding day break out in bright green spots?
Did you ever see a colonel drinking coffee with a horse,
Or a three-legged mongoose? It's very rare, of course.
And if you've never visited a pink giraffe who's sad,
Then you, my friend, are totally, utterly mad!

The Cherry Tree

Once I found a cherry stone,
I put it in the ground,
And when I came to look at it,
A tiny shoot I found.

The shoot grew up and up each day,
And soon became a tree.
I picked the rosy cherries then,
And ate them for my tea.

The Apple Tree

Here is the tree with leaves so green.
Here are the apples that hang between.
When the wind blows the apples fall.
Here is a basket to gather them all.

I Had a Little Nut Tree

I had a little nut tree, nothing would it bear,
But a silver nutmeg, and a golden pear;
The King of Spain's daughter came to visit me,
And all for the sake of my little nut tree.

Little Fishes

Little fishes in a brook,
Father caught them on a hook,
Mother fried them in a pan,
Johnnie eats them like a man.

Ickle Ockle

Ickle ockle, blue bockle,
Fishes in the sea,
If you want a pretty maid,
Please choose me.

I'm a Big Sister!

Ellie was Mummy's and Daddy's little girl. But one day Mummy went into hospital – and when she came back she had a new baby with her.

"Now you're a big sister!" Mummy told Ellie.

Everyone made a big fuss of the new baby.

"Baby's so little!" Auntie Molly said. "Isn't it lovely to be a big sister?"

"Yes," said Ellie. But she wasn't so sure. Sometimes she wished she could be little again, like Baby.

When Baby's nappy needed changing, Ellie asked Mummy, "Did I wear a nappy too?"

Mummy smiled. "Yes you did, Ellie. But now you're too grown-up for nappies. Big sisters wear underpants. Yours have flowers on them."

"And I can put them on myself," said Ellie.

"That's right," said Mummy. "But Baby still needs lots of help – not like you!"

"Can I help change Baby's nappy?" Ellie asked.

"Of course," said Mummy. "Thank you. Baby's very lucky to have a big sister who helps!"

But Ellie still thought it might be fun to be as little as Baby.

The next day, when Daddy got the baby's bottle ready, Ellie asked, "Did I have my dinner in a bottle too?"

Daddy smiled. "Yes, Ellie," he said. "But now you're too grown-up for a bottle. Big sisters eat sandwiches and drink milk from a cup."

"And I can eat sandwiches and drink milk all by myself!" said Ellie. "I don't need anyone to help me."

"Of course you can," said Daddy. "That's what big sisters do. But Baby still needs lots of help."

"Can I help feed the baby?" Ellie asked Daddy.

"I think Baby would like that very much," said Daddy. "Baby's so lucky to have such a helpful big sister!"

That night, Ellie watched Mummy put Baby to sleep.

"Did I sleep in a cot like Baby's?" she asked.

"Yes, Ellie, you did. But now you're too grown-up for a cot," said Mummy. "Big sisters sleep in big, cosy beds, just like yours."

Ellie looked at her bed. With its pretty quilt and a huge pile of cuddly toys, it really did look cosy.

"There are no animals in Baby's cot," Ellie said. "Let's give Baby my yellow bunny – just for now."

"That's very kind of you, Ellie," said Mummy. "Baby is lucky to have a big sister who shares!"

The next day, Ellie and Mummy went out to the park. Baby came too, in a pushchair.

"Did I ride in a pushchair like Baby?" Ellie asked.

"Yes, you did," replied Mummy. "But you're a big sister now. Big sisters can walk – and run and jump. Baby can't do any of those things yet. Baby's lucky to have a strong, big sister like you!"

At the park, Ellie saw the ice-cream van.

"Will you buy an ice cream for Baby?" she asked Mummy.

"No, Ellie," said Mummy. "Baby's too little for ice cream. But her big sister isn't! What flavour would you like?"

"Chocolate!" said Ellie. "Thank you!"

Ellie looked at Baby, and Baby smiled at her.

Ellie smiled too.

"I'm glad we have a baby," she told Mummy. "I get to help, and share and push the pushchair – and I get to have ice cream too! Being a big sister is the best!"

A Friend for Barney

It was Saturday morning at Primrose Farm. Robin, Jenny and Marley the dog went down to the pond to feed some breadcrumbs to the ducks.

"All the ducks are friends," said Jenny. "They never fight about who gets the biggest piece."

"Not like you," said Robin.

"That's because you always get the biggest piece," said Jenny.

When they went to see the chickens, Robin asked, "Are they friends too?"

"I think so," said Jenny, "but some of them are a bit pecky."

"What about the pigs? Sometimes Bessie can be a bit grumpy with her piglets," said Robin.

"Oh, that's just because she is their mum," said Jenny, "and they are very greedy sometimes so Bessie has to tell them off."

"Everybody at Primrose Farm has friends," agreed Robin.

"My best friend is Stan," said Jenny.

"Cats are boring," declared Robin. "They just sleep all the time. My best friend is Marley. He's the fastest dog in the world!"

"But Barney the scarecrow doesn't have a friend," said Jenny, frowning. "He just stands on the hill all day with no one to talk to."

When they went back to the house, Jenny said to her mum, "Barney's lonely."

"Then why don't you make him a friend?" asked Mum. That afternoon she took them to a jumble sale in town so they could get some clothes for a new scarecrow. Robin found an old pair of sports shoes and a pair of motorbike gloves. Jenny found a pink party dress and a hat with a green ribbon.

Robin stuffed an old sack with straw and Dad helped Jenny to paint a face at the top. Mum made some hair out of wool.

"What a beauty," said Dad. "All she needs is a name."

"I want to call her Mary, like my favourite doll," said Jenny.

"Scary Mary Crow," said Robin. "That's a great name."

So, that's what they called her. They took Scary Mary up the hill.

"Hello, Barney," said Robin. "We've brought you a friend."

"Now you won't be lonely any more," added Jenny.

"I think Barney likes her," said Robin. "He can see by looking at the shoes she's wearing that she's very good at football."

"I think he likes her because she has a smiley face," said Jenny.

Jenny skipped all the way home to tell Stan the cat all about Scary Mary. "I'm very happy, Stan," she said, giving him a big hug. "Now everybody at Primrose Farm has a friend."

Nibbling Neighbours

One sunny morning in the meadow, Alice was happily munching away when she was surprised to discover a hole where there should be grass.

"My dears," she mooed, "there's a hole in our field!"

The next morning, where there had been one hole before, now there were five!

"If this goes on," said Bryony, "we'll have nowhere to stand!"

"And nothing to eat," added Rowan, sounding alarmed.

By the end of the week, there were over a hundred holes.

"You've got some nibbling neighbours," said Farmer Jim. "It looks like a family of rabbits has come to stay."

The cows shuddered. "Those hopping things with long ears?" asked Holly. "I can't look my best with them around!"

"And they have very, very large families," warned Rowan. "Not just one baby at a time, like cows do."

"It's odd we've never seen one," said Bryony thoughtfully. "I'm going to keep watch tonight."

That night, as the full moon rose over the meadow, Bryony pretended to go to sleep.

Although she was expecting it, she was shocked when two bright eyes and a twitchy nose popped up in front of her.

"*Aaaaaghh!*" cried Bryony.

"*Aaaaaghh!*" cried the rabbit, and disappeared down its hole.

"You should have followed it!" cried Alice, who had been woken by the sudden noise.

"Down a rabbit hole?" gasped Rowan. "Don't be silly, Alice. She's far too big!"

"Then we're doomed," said Holly, gloomily. "Those rabbits will take over without us even seeing them do it."

The next morning, the cows awoke to an amazing sight. Hundreds of rabbits were sitting around them.

"Excuse me!" said the largest one. "We've come to ask for your help."

"Help?" echoed Alice. "We're the ones who need help!"

The rabbit explained that his family lived in fear. "Your hoofs are so big, you could stamp on us without noticing."

Just then, Bryony had one of her excellent ideas. "You would be much safer," she said, "if you lived under the hedgerow."

So they did. All day in the meadow, there's munching and mooing. All night in the hedgerow, there's nibbling, digging and wiggling. And everyone is happy.

My Mother Said

My mother said I never should
Play with the gypsies in the wood.

If I did, then she would say:
"Naughty girl to disobey!

Your hair shan't curl and your shoes shan't shine,
You gypsy girl, you won't be mine!"

The wood was dark; the grass was green;
In came Sally with a tambourine.

I crept to the sea – no ship to get across;
I paid ten shillings for a blind white horse.

I got up on his back and was off in a crack.
Sally, tell my mother I shall never come back.

Bed in Summer

In winter I get up at night
And dress by yellow candle-light.
In summer quite the other way,
I have to go to bed by day.

I have to go to bed and see
The birds still hopping on the tree,
Or hear the grown-up people's feet
Still going past me in the street.

And does it not seem hard to you,
When all the sky is clear and blue,
And I should like so much to play,
To have to go to bed by day?

Snoozy Princess Susie

Z-Z-Z-zz

Princess Susie was quite perfect in almost every way.
She always fed her dragon, Spark, and put her clothes away.
She never ever said rude words, or disobeyed the queen.
Her bedroom was the tidiest that you have ever seen!

But Susie did do something that made her mother weep.
No matter what the time of day, poor Susie fell asleep!
She fell asleep at breakfast, and in the banquet hall.
She often dozed upon the stairs, all curled up in a ball.

The queen was beside herself. "The answer's plain," she said.
"If Susie just can't keep awake, she must go straight to bed!"
But though she went to bed at six, and didn't rise till nine,
Susie yawned and snored all day, no matter what the time.

No one knew quite what to do to put the matter right,
Till clever fairy Heather saw something strange one night.
As she flew home in the dark she heard a gentle sigh.
There was Susie, wide awake, gazing at the sky!

"I love to watch the stars," she said, "and see the shining moon!
I'd rather be here, counting stars, than sleeping in my room!"
Heather smiled and waved her wand. "I have a plan!" she said.
As if by magic shining stars appeared above the bed.

Now Susie watches stars in bed to help her get to sleep.
She counts them as they float above, instead of counting sheep!

Birthday Sleepover

It was Ali's birthday and she had invited her friends to a special sleepover. As it was a warm summer evening, they were going to camp in the garden in Ali's new tent. They had been looking forward to it for weeks and were planning a special midnight feast.

The moon was shining brightly as the girls settled into the tent. Ali, Martha and Daisy zipped up the door and climbed into their sleeping bags.

"It's such a pity Ashley couldn't come," said Martha. "This is going to be so much fun!"

They unpacked their feast of crisps, biscuits and chocolate-spread sandwiches. As they tucked in, they made each other laugh with spooky ghost stories.

Daisy began telling them about an old barn nearby. Her brother had said it was haunted.

Then there was a bang from outside the tent.

"What was that?" asked Martha, looking worried.

"Just a cat, or something," said Ali, nervously.

They all listened again. There was another bang and then a noise that sounded like a twig snapping. Martha jumped. "That wasn't a cat!" she said, grabbing her torch.

"What's that strange rustling noise?" said Daisy.

Ali reached for her shoes. "I don't like this one bit!" she said.

"Let's get out of here!" yelled Daisy.

The girls grabbed their things and squeezed out of the tent.

"Quick! Follow me!" shouted Ali. She began to lead them across the grass towards the summerhouse.

"Wait!" said a voice behind them. "Where are you all going?" It was Ashley!

"My mum said I could come after all!" Ashley laughed. "But it was hard to find your tent in the dark."

Ali, Daisy and Martha laughed. "So it was you making all those noises!" said Daisy. "Not a ghost at all!"

Ali hugged Ashley. "I'm so glad you're here," she said. "It wouldn't have been a proper birthday without you."

"Now let's finish off this midnight feast!" cried Martha.

The Enchanted Garden

Princess Sylvie loved to walk through the meadows to look at the flowers.

One day she found an overgrown path in her favourite meadow. She asked a woman where the path led.

"To the garden of the enchantress!" said the woman. "You can go and look, but they say that whatever you do, don't pick the flowers."

Princess Sylvie followed the path until she came to a cottage with the prettiest garden she had ever seen, filled with flowers of every colour and perfume.

Princess Sylvie went back to the garden every day. Soon she forgot all about the enchantress – and one day, she picked a rose from the garden and took it back to the castle. As she put it in water, Princess Sylvie suddenly remembered the warning!

But months passed and nothing happened. The rose stayed as fresh as the day it was picked. Forgetting her fears, Princess Sylvie went back to the enchanted garden.

When she saw the garden, Princess Sylvie wanted to cry. The grass was brown. All the flowers had withered.

Then she heard someone weeping. Inside the cottage the enchantress was sitting by the fire, crying. She was old and bent. Princess Sylvie was afraid, but she felt sorry for her.

"What happened to your lovely garden?" Princess Sylvie asked.

"Someone picked a rose from it!" said the enchantress. "The garden is under a spell: the picked flower will live forever, but the rest of the flowers must die! And when the rose was picked, my magic was lost, too, and I too am beginning to wither and die!"

"What can I do?" said Princess Sylvie, heartbroken.

"Only a princess can help," she replied. "She must bring me six sacks of stinging nettles! And no princess would do that!"

Princess Sylvie gathered six sacks of nettles, not caring that they stung her, and took them back to the enchantress.

The enchantress said, "But the nettles must be picked by a princess."

"I am a princess," said Princess Sylvie.

The enchantress made a magic potion with the nettles and drank it. Instantly, the garden became beautiful again – and Princess Sylvie gasped! Gone was the bent old lady. In her place was a beautiful young woman.

"My garden is restored," smiled the enchantress, "and so am I!"

And so the enchantress and the princess became great friends and shared the enchanted garden.

Can I See Another's Woe?

Can I see another's woe,
And not be in sorrow, too?
Can I see another's grief,
And not seek for kind relief?

Bob Robin

Little Bob Robin,
Where do you live?
Up in yonder wood, sir,
On a hazel twig.

Old Farmer Giles

Old Farmer Giles,
He went seven miles
With his faithful dog Old Rover;
And his faithful dog Old Rover,
When he came to the stiles,
Took a run, and jumped clean over.

Red Stockings

Red stockings, blue stockings,
Shoes tied up with silver;
A red rosette upon my breast
And a gold ring on my finger.

Fidget

As little Jenny Wren
Was sitting by the shed,
She waggled with her tail,
She nodded with her head;
She waggled with her tail,
She nodded with her head;
As Little Jenny Wren
Was sitting by the shed.

The Dove Says

The dove says, "Coo, coo! What shall I do?
I can scarce maintain two."
"Pooh, pooh," says the wren, "I have ten,
And keep them all like gentlemen.
Curr dhoo, curr dhoo! Love me and I'll love you!"

Dreams

Beyond, beyond the mountain line,
The grey-stone and the boulder,
Beyond the growth of dark green pine,
That crowns its western shoulder,
There lies that fairy land of mine,
Unseen of a beholder.

Its fruits are all like rubies rare,
Its streams are clear as glasses:
There golden castles hang in air,
And purple grapes in masses,
And noble knights and ladies fair
Come riding down the passes.

Ah me! They say if I could stand
Upon those mountain ledges,
I should but see on either hand
Plain fields and dusty hedges:
And yet I know my fairy land
Lies somewhere o'er their hedges.

Three Little Kittens

Three little kittens,
They lost their mittens,
And they began to cry,
"Oh, mother dear,
We sadly fear
Our mittens we have lost."

"What? Lost your mittens,
You naughty kittens!
Then you shall have no pie.
Miaow, miaow, miaow, miaow.
No, you shall have no pie."

The three little kittens,
They found their mittens,
And they began to smile,
"Oh, mother dear,
See here, see here,
Our mittens we have found."

"What? Found your mittens,
You clever kittens!
Then you shall have some pie.
Purr, purr, purr, purr.
Oh, let us have some pie."

My Dad Is Great

My dad is great. We have brilliant fun together.

Today, Mum and Baby are going shopping with Grandma for the day, so Dad and I have all day to spend together. I'm so excited!

I can't wait to see what adventures Dad has planned for me while they're away.

My dad is very patient. He always lets me choose all of my own clothes.

He doesn't care how long it takes. I think that, secretly, he quite enjoys it! (I wonder if he would like me to help choose his clothes?)

My dad often picks me up from school. He's bigger and stronger than all the other dads.

And he's a fantastic sailor. He's got a smashing white yacht.

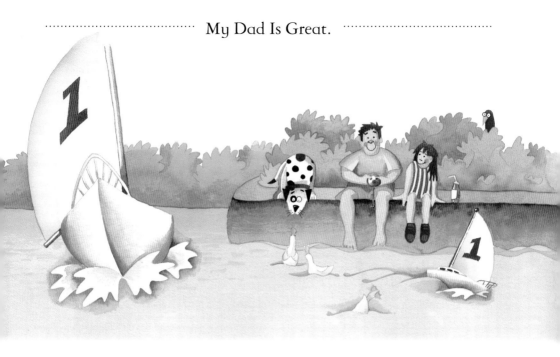

It's the fastest boat on the pond in the park down the road.

He's a great sport. He always lets me win when we play football. (But I pretend not to notice.)

Dad and I like the same things. Hot dogs are our very favourite food in the whole wide world.

My dad's ever so funny. He always makes me laugh.

My dad's a brilliant runner. He runs around the park much quicker than everyone else.

When Dad's around, everything seems fun.

Even washing up and tidying up!

When they get home, I tell Mum and Baby about the amazing things we've been doing. I can't wait until Baby is old enough to hear all about Dad.

Because although all dads are special, my dad is… *great*!

An Angel of My Own

Lizzie was a pretty little girl who lived with her mum, her dad and her baby brother Matthew.

Lizzie looked as good and sweet as a little angel, but she didn't always act like one. Sometimes, she could be very naughty indeed.

One afternoon, Lizzie's grandma came for tea. Grandma was very pleased to see Lizzie and baby Matthew.

"Lizzie, please kiss your grandma hello," said Mum. But Lizzie ran away from Grandma into the garden.

Later that evening, Lizzie wanted to play.

"Please play quietly, Lizzie," Mum said. "Matthew is asleep."

But Lizzie started jumping loudly across the floor.

Stamp! Stamp! Stamp! went Lizzie's feet. Matthew woke up and began to cry.

"Stop crying, Matthew," ordered Lizzie. She pulled a face at him. Matthew cried even harder.

"Please be nice to Matthew," Mum said, when she saw what Lizzie was doing. Lizzie stuck out her tongue rudely.

That night, Lizzie felt unhappy. She thought about all the naughty things she'd done. She wished she could make everything all right.

In the middle of the night, Lizzie was sleeping peacefully.

Suddenly, a strange glow filled the room. Lizzie opened her eyes and next to her bed was a beautiful angel. The angel had a kind face and wonderful, shimmering wings.

"Hello, Lizzie," smiled the angel. "Don't be afraid. I know that you're feeling a bit sad. I've come to try and help you."

The angel took Lizzie by the hand. "Let's talk about all the things that have happened today, and think about how we could have made them better. It would make your grandma so happy if you would spend time with her."

"I didn't mean to run away from Grandma," said Lizzie.

"And what about baby Matthew?" asked the angel. "If you accidentally wake him up, why don't you try and make him laugh instead of cry?"

Lizzie nodded her head happily. That was a good idea. Lizzie felt much better.

The angel tucked Lizzie back into bed and stroked her face tenderly.

"I wish I could be a beautiful angel like you one day," Lizzie whispered.

The angel smiled. "Well Lizzie, you have to be very good to become an angel," she replied. "But I'm sure you can do it if you try."

Lizzie nodded her head. "Yes, I think I can," she said. "I'll be much nicer from now on."

The next afternoon, Lizzie's grandma came to tea. Without being asked, Lizzie ran up to her and gave her a big kiss.

"Hello, Lizzie!" said Grandma happily. "It's lovely to see you."

Lizzie and Grandma had a wonderful time. Lizzie drew Grandma a special picture, which she was very pleased with. Then they played lots of nice games together.

At teatime, everyone enjoyed all the lovely food Lizzie's mum had made.

That evening, after Grandma had gone home, Lizzie wanted to play.

"Please play quietly," said Mum. "Matthew's sleeping."

Lizzie had wanted to play noisily. She started to jump across the floor, but then remembered what the angel had said.

Matthew hadn't woken up, so Lizzie tiptoed silently across the room and chose a book from the shelf. She sat quietly on a bean bag to look at it.

Lizzie didn't make a single sound.

As the days and weeks passed by, Lizzie was hardly naughty at all.

One day, Mum and Dad had a special surprise for her.

"We're very proud of you," said Dad, giving Lizzie a big hug. "You've been such a good girl lately, we've got you a present."

Dad handed Lizzie a box. Inside was a beautiful silver necklace. There was an angel charm hanging from it.

"A little angel for our little angel," said Mum. She put the necklace around Lizzie's neck.

"Oh! Thank you, Mum!" beamed Lizzie as she gave her mum a great big hug.

The Seasons

In the winter comes the snow,
Makes our feet and fingers glow.
Early spring brings the rain,
Thaws the frozen ponds again.
Then come breezes, loud and shrill,
They stir the dancing daffodil.
Soon flowers the primrose sweet,
Daisies scatter at our feet.
See the flocks of pretty lambs,
Skipping by their fleecy dams!
Summer brings tulips, lilies, roses;
Fills the children's hands and posies.
Then it brings us cooling showers,
Strawberries and gilly-flowers.
The sun ripens sheaves of corn,
Then the harvest home is borne.
In the autumn comes the pheasant;
Then to gather nuts is pleasant.
But all too soon come icy blasts,
Then the leaves are falling fast.
In the winter comes the snow,
Makes our feet and fingers glow.

The Moon

The moon has a face like the clock in the hall;
She shines on thieves on the garden wall,
On streets and fields and harbour quays,
And birdies asleep in the forks of the trees.

The squalling cat and the squeaking mouse,
The howling dog by the door of the house,
The bat that lies in bed at noon,
All love to be out by the light of the moon.

But all of the things that belong to the day
Cuddle to sleep to be out of her way;
And flowers and children close their eyes
Till up in the morning the sun shall arise.

In Lincoln Lane

I lost my mare in Lincoln Lane,
I'll never find her there again;
She lost a shoe, and then lost two,
And threw her rider in the drain.

Charley Barley

Charley Barley, butter and eggs,
Sold his wife for three duck eggs.
When the ducks began to lay,
Charley Barley flew away.

Five Little Ducks

Five little ducks went swimming one day,
Over the hills and far away,
Mother Duck said, "Quack, quack, quack, quack,"
But only four little ducks came back.
Four little ducks went swimming one day,
Over the hills and far away,
Mother Duck said, "Quack, quack, quack, quack,"
But only three little ducks came back.

(continue with three little ducks, etc.)

There Was an Old Crow

There was an old crow
Sat upon a clod:
There's an end of my song,
That's odd!

Birds of a Feather

Birds of a feather flock together,
And so will pigs and swine;
Rats and mice shall have their choice,
And so shall I have mine.

The Wise Old Owl

There was an old owl who lived in an oak;
The more he heard, the less he spoke.
The less he spoke, the more he heard.
Why aren't we like that wise old bird?

Sleepover Splash

In Ashley's bedroom Martha, Daisy and Ali were rolling out their sleeping bags for another sleepover.

"Max is driving me mad!" said Ashley. "I hate having a twin brother!"

All day long Max had been playing jokes on Ashley. He and his friend James had put a frog in her bed and spread mustard in her peanut-butter sandwiches. They had also hidden her ballet shoes so she was late for her lesson.

"Why don't you get your own back?" said Martha. She sat down on Ashley's bed. "Let's come up with a really good joke to play on him!"

"I know!" said Daisy. "Here's a good joke! Let's put a bucket of water above his door. When he opens it he'll get soaked!"

"That's a great idea!" said Ashley, jumping up. "I'll go and get a bucket from downstairs and you all make sure Max is out of his room!"

Martha and Ali went out onto the

landing and knocked on Max's door. There was no answer. "All clear!" they called. Ashley came back up with the bucket, and she and Daisy took it to the bathroom to fill it with water.

Daisy climbed onto a chair and lifted up the bucket.

Ashley opened Max's door just enough so the bucket would balance on top. "Max!" she called. "There's something in your room for you!"

Ashley, Ali and Martha raced across the landing, back to Ashley's bedroom. "Quick, Daisy!" hissed Ashley.

But just as Max came up the stairs, Daisy lost her balance on the chair and, with a loud cry, tumbled down onto Max. The bucket toppled over, soaking them both from head to toe in icy-cold water!

Mina's Lucky Shoes

Mina loved ballet. She went to the Starlight Ballet School. She had a ballet class every week.

Mina loved her ballet teacher, Miss Silver.

"You dance very well, Mina," said Miss Silver.

Mina was very happy – except for one thing. She found one of the dance steps very hard! When Mina had to spin around very fast it made her dizzy. Sometimes she even fell over!

"Try again, Mina," said Miss Silver. "Keep your head in one place as you are spinning, and then turn it round quickly at the last minute. You will do it."

Mina tried again, but she just couldn't get the hang of it. Spinning still made her dizzy.

"I'll never be able to spin," she said sadly to her mum.

"I have an idea," said Mum. She went up to the attic. When she came back down again she was holding an old box.

She gave the box to Mina. There were some yellow ballet shoes inside. They were made of the most beautiful satin, but they were very old.

"Wow!" said Mina. "Whose are these?"

"These were my lucky ballet shoes when I was your age," said her mum.

Mina put on the yellow ballet shoes. They fitted perfectly.

Then she tried a spin. She thought hard about what Miss Silver had told her. She turned her head at the last minute. And Mina didn't feel dizzy!

"They are lucky!" she said to Mum.

Mum laughed. "Maybe they are," she said. "That's what I used to think. But maybe you've just learnt how to spin."

"They are definitely lucky," said Mina.

Mina wore the yellow ballet shoes for her next class. Her spinning was perfect.

"Well done, Mina," said Miss Silver, when she saw Mina spinning around the dance studio.

Mina was delighted!

Good Girl, Molly

Molly's mum Meg was a sheepdog. She helped Farmer Peter round up the sheep.

"Good girl, Meg," Peter would say almost every day.

Molly was too small to help. Whenever she tried to help, Farmer Peter would say, "Stay here, Molly."

Molly was bored of watching Mum round up sheep. She wanted to help, too. She wanted Farmer Peter to say, "Good girl, Molly," to her, too.

One day, Meg was helping Farmer Peter to put all the sheep into a big pen.

"Good girl, Meg," said Farmer Peter, closing the gate and patting Meg on the head. But as he turned away a lamb slipped through the last crack in the gate and ran away.

Meg did not see. But Molly saw the lamb. She ran after it.

"Where is Molly?" said Farmer Peter, a few minutes later.

Then he heard barking coming from the top field.

The naughty lamb had got itself stuck in a hedge. Farmer Peter saw Molly barking next to the lamb.

"Good girl, Molly," he said.

Goldy and the Jacket

"Naughty Goldy!" Susie the farmer would cry almost every day, as she came out to get the washing to find the goat munching on a tea towel or chomping on a sock.

But Goldy wouldn't stop. She just loved eating washing!

One day there was a green jacket hanging on the line.

"Tasty!" thought Goldy. Soon she had munched it all up.

It wasn't long before Goldy started to feel ill.

"Has she eaten anything unusual?" the vet asked Susie.

Susie gasped. "My waterproof jacket! When I brought the clothes in it had gone. She must have eaten it. Poor Goldy!"

The vet laughed. "Goats have tough stomachs," he said. "She'll soon feel better." He patted Goldy on the head. "And that'll teach you to eat things goats aren't supposed to eat!"

"Baaa!" agreed Goldy.

Just as the vet said, Goldy was soon feeling better.

"Grass is enough for me from now on!" she said to herself, chewing a mouthful. "No more laundry for Goldy."

Then she looked over at the washing line. There was a yummy-looking red sock hanging on it.

"Well, maybe just one last sock..." she thought.

Fishes Swim

Fishes swim in water clear,
Birds fly up into the air,
Serpents creep along the ground,
Boys and girls run round and round.

Feathers

Cackle, cackle, Mother Goose,
Have you any feathers loose?
Truly have I, pretty fellow,
Half enough to fill a pillow.
Here are quills, take one or two,
And down to make a bed for you.

Cut Thistles

Cut thistles in May,
They'll grow in a day;
Cut them in June,
That is too soon;
Cut them in July,
Then they will die.

Pussycat and Robin

Little Robin Redbreast sat upon a tree,
Up went pussycat, and down went he!
Down came pussy, and away Robin ran;
Says little Robin Redbreast,
"Catch me if you can!"

Robin and Pussycat

Little Robin Redbreast jumped upon a wall,
Pussycat jumped after him,
And almost got a fall!
Little Robin chirped and sang,
And what did pussy say?
Pussycat said, "Mew,"
And Robin jumped away.

Three Blind Mice

Three blind mice, three blind mice!
See how they run, see how they run!
They all ran after the farmer's wife,
Who cut off their tails with a carving-knife,
Did ever you see such a thing in your life,
As three blind mice?

Bedtime

The evening is coming, the sun sinks to rest;
The rooks are all flying straight home to the nest.
"Caw!" says the rook, as he flies overhead;
"It's time little people were going to bed!"

The flowers are closing; the daisy's asleep;
The primrose is buried in slumber so deep.
Shut up for the night is the Pimpernel red;
It's time little people were going to bed!

The butterfly, drowsy, has folded its wing;
The bees are returning, no more the birds sing.
Their labour is over, their nestlings are fed;
It's time little people were going to bed!

Hush, Little Baby

Hush, little baby, don't say a word,
Papa's gonna buy you a mockingbird.

If that mocking bird don't sing,
Papa's gonna buy you a diamond ring.

If that diamond ring turns brass,
Papa's gonna buy you a looking glass.

If that looking glass gets broke,
Papa's gonna buy you a billy goat.

If that billy goat don't pull,
Papa's gonna buy you a cart and bull.

If that cart and bull turn over,
Papa's gonna buy you a dog named Rover.

And if that dog named Rover won't bark.
Papa's gonna to buy you and horse and cart.

And if that horse and cart fall down,
You'll still be the sweetest little baby in town.

197

The Case of the Disappearing Books

It was the hottest summer Molly could remember. She'd walked to the libary on an errand for her mum.

"I'd like a book about baking cakes," she told Miss Brown, the librarian.

Miss Brown shook her head. "Sorry, Molly. A lot of the books have gone missing." She pointed to a big gap on a shelf.

"All the books in the library have disappeared!" said Molly, when she got home.

"Never mind," said Molly's mum. "It's too hot to cook anyway." She gave Molly a cool drink. "Your friend Tiffany phoned and she's invited you over to her house this afternoon."

"Oh, great!" Molly said, forgetting all about the missing books.

Tiffany lived in a big house just outside the village. Her dad was Freddy Parker – he had been a famous rock star a long time ago.

When Molly arrived

at Tiffany's house, Tiffany's dad was complaining about the hot weather. All the doors in the house were open to keep the rooms cool. Molly's eyes widened as she saw that they were wedged open with books.

She opened one. It was a library book. Molly looked around. At least fifty library books were propping open the doors!

"Look, Tiffany," she whispered.

Tiffany turned to her dad. "Daddy! You can't take this many books from the library, just because you're famous!" she scolded.

"I guess you're right, Tiff," Freddy said sheepishly. "Let's take the books back."

Freddy, Tiffany and Molly staggered into the library carrying armfuls of books.

"Hey, sorry I borrowed your books without asking," Freddy said to Miss Brown. "Why don't you come over for a swim?" He gave Miss Brown his famous smile.

Miss Brown was very pleased to get her books back. But she was even more pleased to meet her favourite rock star.

An hour or so later, Miss Brown was sipping a cool drink with Freddy, as Molly and Tiffany splashed about in the Parker Heights pool.

"This is the life!" Molly heard her say.

Perfect Pony

Pepper thought that he was the luckiest pony on the whole of Merrymead Farm. He wasn't the most handsome, the smartest or even the fastest pony but Pepper didn't mind one bit. He knew he was the luckiest pony on the farm because Lucy owned him.

Lucy was never cross or mean and always took Pepper for the nicest of rides. She ignored the other children and their ponies when they laughed at Pepper for knocking down the odd jump or for going slower than everyone else.

"They're just jealous," she'd whisper. "Because you're the best pony on the whole farm." And most of the time, Pepper managed to believe her. After all, Lucy was always right.

One summer evening, Lucy rushed out to the meadow with a piece of paper in her hand.

"Look, Pepper," she cried. "There's going to be a gymkhana tomorrow right here on Merrymead Farm! There are going to be games and jumping and even a showing class. I can't wait. I know that we're going to win lots of lovely rosettes."

As Lucy rushed off to spread the news, the other ponies in the meadow started to snicker.

"Oh dear!" laughed Bluey, the largest of the ponies. "I don't think you're built for jumping."

"Your legs are too short to go fast," said Swallow, the quickest pony on the farm.

"You're far too scruffy for showing," said Ebony, the sleek and vain show pony.

That night, Pepper lay awake worrying about the gymkhana. "The other ponies are right," he thought. "I'm no good for anything. I'm bound to let Lucy down at the gymkhana."

As these thoughts tumbled through his head, Pepper fell into a restless, dream-filled sleep. He dreamt that a beautiful white horse appeared before him. "I am the Great White Horse," she whispered. "I've come to help you."

Pepper blinked as she called, "Fly with me to see the best pony on Merrymead Farm."

Pepper felt his hoofs lift from the ground.

"*Whooaah,*" he cried,

waggling his legs as he soared through the sky.

"Now look below you," said the Great White Horse.

Pepper looked down on a familiar scene. "It's the farm," he cried. "And look, Lucy and I are trotting past the geese."

"Yes, and look at all the other ponies," said the Great White Horse. "While you march past the geese without any fuss, they shake with fear or run away."

The Great White Horse reared up and tossed her flowing mane and the scene beneath them changed.

Pepper watched as the children got their ponies ready for a ride. He couldn't help smiling as he watched himself and Lucy rubbing noses. That was one of their favourite games.

Behind Lucy, Pepper could see Bluey putting back his ears and waving his back leg at his little boy.

"Ooh! That's not nice," gasped Pepper.

"Exactly," said the Great White Horse. "Pepper, you are brave, loyal and kind. You are the perfect pony for Lucy. Just be yourself tomorrow and everything will be all right!"

In the gymkhana the next day the first class was the jumping. Pepper set off at a steady trot. Slowly but surely he sailed clear over each jump.

"Nearly there," he thought, as he launched himself at the last jump. But his back hoof tapped the pole and it rattled to the ground. Pepper couldn't believe his bad luck. But Lucy was delighted, particularly when she was given a red rosette for coming fourth.

In the egg and spoon race, Pepper trotted so steadily that Lucy didn't drop her egg once. Lucy was over the moon when they were given a yellow rosette for coming third.

And they did even better in the pole-bending race, even though Pepper's round belly made it rather difficult to bend quickly round the poles.

"Well done," said the judge, as she awarded Pepper a beautiful blue rosette for coming second.

The final event of the day was the showing class.

"All the other ponies are smarter than me," thought Pepper. But as he trotted round, he remembered the words of the Great White Horse and began to relax. He was so busy enjoying himself that it took a few seconds to realize that the judge was saying something.

"And the winners are Pepper and Lucy," the judge said, pinning a green rosette to Pepper's bridle.

Lucy laughed in delight and rubbed noses with Pepper. Pepper gasped. Then he looked up at the sky.

"Thank you, Great White Horse," he whispered.

Oranges and Lemons

Oranges and lemons,
Say the bells of St Clements.
I owe you five farthings,
Say the bells of St Martins.
When will you pay me?
Say the bells of Old Bailey.
When I grow rich,
Say the bells of Shoreditch.

London Bells

Gay go up and gay go down,
To ring the bells of London town.
Halfpence and farthings,
Say the bells of St Martin's.
Pancakes and fritters,
Say the bells of St Peter's.
Two sticks and an apple,
Say the bells of Whitechapel.

My Little Cow

I had a little cow,
Hey diddle, ho diddle!
I had a little cow, and I drove it to the stall;
Hey diddle, ho diddle! And there's my song all.

Jemmy Dawson

Brave news is come to town,
Brave news is carried;
Brave news is come to town,
Jemmy Dawson's married.

I See the Moon

I see the moon,
And the moon sees me;
God bless the moon,
And God bless me.

For Every Evil Under the Sun

For every evil under the sun,
There is a remedy, or there is none.
If there be one, try and find it;
If there be none, never mind it.

Lucy's Big Chance

The Starlight Ballet School was putting on a show.

Lucy wanted to dance in the show so she tried very hard to dance well in class. She concentrated as hard as she could and she practised her ballet steps at home every single night.

Miss Silver was delighted with the way Lucy had been dancing.

"I'm going to give you the role of the fairy queen, Lucy," she said, giving Lucy a pink and yellow dress.

Lucy looked at the dress. It looked very big. But she didn't say anything to Miss Silver because she wanted to be the fairy queen more than anything in the world.

When Lucy tried on the dress at home her worst fears were realized. It was much too big!

"Oh, no!" thought Lucy. She was worried. She was worried that Miss Silver might give the part to a bigger girl.

Just then Lucy's mum called her for tea.

"Coming, Mum!" said Lucy. She took off her dress and went downstairs.

"Where's your dress, Lucy?" asked Miss Silver at the next ballet class, when they were rehearsing for the show.

"I forgot it, Miss Silver," said Lucy.

Her face felt hot and red.

"Just make sure you don't forget it for the show," said Miss Silver. Lucy looked down. She felt very bad. The dress was too big and she knew that she had told a lie.

On the way home, Lucy knew what she must do. "I will tell Mum," she thought.

"Mum, I need to..." she said, as soon as she got home. But before she could continue Mum interrupted her.

"Lucy, I'm so sorry. Your lovely dress has shrunk in the wash!" she said.

Lucy smiled to herself. She went upstairs and tried on the dress again.

It was the perfect fit!

Let's Play!

Molly wanted to play.

"Let's play, Hetty," said Molly.

"Not today, Molly," said Hetty the horse.

"But it's so nice and sunny, Hetty," said Molly. "Perfect weather for playing!"

"Not today, Molly," said Hetty.

"I have a new ball!" said Molly to Hetty. "All the more reason to play. Come on!"

"Not today, Molly," said Hetty.

The vet came to see Hetty later that day.

Molly waited and waited outside the stable. She waited for hours. Finally the vet came out, followed by the farmer.

Then Hetty came out. But behind her Molly could see someone else. It was a new foal!

"This is Twinkle," said Hetty proudly.

"Hello, Twinkle," said Molly.

"Hello, Molly," said Twinkle.

"Now we can all play together!" said Hetty.

This Is Fun!

Chucky the hen was in the barn sitting on her egg. She sighed to herself. "Sitting on eggs is boring," she thought.

Then Dotty the duck waddled past.

"I'm going to the pond to swim," said Dotty. "Come along!"

"Okay!" said Chucky.

At the pond, Dotty began swimming. "This is fun!" she said.

"Now or never," thought Chucky. She jumped in. It was freezing! It was wet! There was slimy green duckweed everywhere!

Chucky had forgotten that ducks are designed for swimming on ponds. They have warm, waterproof feathers and webbed feet and they like slimy green duckweed.

Hens are not designed for swimming on ponds.

Chucky coughed and spluttered and flapped her wings. Finally she managed to scramble out of the pond.

"I'm going home," she shivered.

Chucky sat on her egg. The barn was lovely and warm.

"Now this is fun!" clucked Chucky.

Twinkle, Twinkle

Twinkle, twinkle, little star,
How I wonder what you are!
Up above the world so high,
Like a diamond in the sky.

When the blazing sun is gone,
When he nothing shines upon,
Then you show your little light,
Twinkle, twinkle, all the night.

Then the traveller in the dark,
Thanks you for your tiny spark,
He could not see which way to go,
If you did not twinkle so.

As your bright and tiny spark,
Lights the traveller in the dark –
Though I know not what you are,
Twinkle, twinkle, little star.

Sleep, Baby, Sleep

Sleep, baby, sleep,
Your father keeps the sheep;
Your mother shakes the dreamland tree
And from it fall sweet dreams for thee;
Sleep, baby, sleep.

Sleep, baby, sleep,
The large stars are the sheep;
The little stars are the lambs, I guess,
And the gentle moon is the shepherdess;
Sleep, baby, sleep.

Sleep, baby, sleep,
Your father keeps the sheep;
Your mother guards the lambs this night,
And keeps them safe till morning light;
Sleep, baby, sleep.

My Best Friend

Emily was playing in the back garden with her favourite doll, Hannah.

"Hello, Emily!" called a cheerful voice.

It was Sarah, who lived next door. The two girls were best friends.

"Can I play with Hannah, too?" asked Sarah, reaching out to pick her up.

Emily held on tightly to Hannah. She was a very special doll, and Emily didn't like anybody else to play with her.

"Hannah's tired," said Emily. "I think I'll put her to bed. Then I'll come back and play with you."

For the rest of the morning, Emily and Sarah played in Emily's treehouse. It was their special hideout, and nobody else was allowed in it.

They both thought it was great living next door to one another.

The next day, both girls got up early and ran down to the front garden. They were very excited. They were going on holiday together. Every year, they went to the same holiday cottage. Sarah was travelling with Emily's family. That way they could talk to each other on the journey.

"Can Hannah sit between us?" Sarah asked Emily as they climbed into the car.

"Sorry," said Emily. "Hannah says she wants to sit by the window." And she tucked Hannah safely out of Sarah's reach.

At last they arrived at the cottage, and the girls raced from room to room checking that nothing had changed since last year. At bedtime, they snuggled down in their cosy beds in the attic. They loved sharing a room on holiday. They stayed awake long after the lights went out, talking and laughing together.

This holiday was the best one yet. One day Sarah rode her bicycle without stabilizers for the first time. The next day Emily did the same. Soon the girls were racing each other.

"Can we carry on racing each other when we get home?" Sarah asked her mum and dad. Her mum frowned.

"Hmmm," she began. "There's something we've been meaning to tell you. We're moving away. Daddy's got a new job, and we've found a wonderful new house."

Emily and Sarah couldn't believe their ears. They wouldn't be neighbours any more!

"It's not too far. You'll still be able to see Emily at weekends and during holidays," Dad said.

"But I don't want to move!" cried Sarah. She threw her arms around Emily. "You won't forget me, will you?" she whispered.

Back at home after the holiday, the last days of the summer flew by. On the morning that Sarah and her family were due to leave, Emily and her parents came outside to say goodbye.

"I've brought you a present to remember me by," said Sarah, handing Emily the gift. Emily ripped off the paper. Nestled inside was a gorgeous golden heart necklace.

"It's beautiful!" Emily smiled. Then she rushed inside her house. She came out a minute later carrying Hannah.

"Here," she said, putting the doll into Sarah's arms. "Hannah will keep you company until you make friends at your new house."

Sarah was speechless. She gave Emily an enormous hug.

Emily grinned. "Sharing really is great," she declared. "Especially sharing things with your very best friend."

Frère Jacques

Frère Jacques, Frère Jacques,
Dormez-vous, dormez-vous?
Sonnez les matines, sonnez les matines,
Ding, dang, dong, ding, dang, dong.

O Lady Moon

O Lady Moon, your horns point toward the east:
Shine, be increased.
O Lady Moon, your horns point toward the west:
Wane, be at rest.

Ding, Dong, Bell

Ding, dong, bell,
Pussy's in the well!
Who put her in?
Little Tommy Green.
Who pulled her out?
Little Johnny Stout.
What a naughty boy was that
To try to drown poor pussycat,
Who never did any harm,
But killed the mice in his father's barn.

Muffin Man

Have you seen the muffin man,
The muffin man, the muffin man,
Have you seen the muffin man
That lives in Drury Lane, O?

The Coachman

Up at Piccadilly, O!
The coachman takes his stand,
And when he meets a pretty girl,
He takes her by the hand;
Whip away for ever, O!
Drive away so clever, O!
All the way to Bristol, O!
He drives her four-in-hand.

The Miller of Dee

There was a jolly miller
Lived on the river Dee:
He worked and sang from morn till night,
No lark so blithe as he;
And this the burden of his song for ever used to be:
I jump me jerrime jee!
I care for nobody – no! not I,
Since nobody cares for me.

The Case of the Disgusting Doughnuts

"One doughnut, please," Molly said. She handed her money to Mr Jones, the baker. Mr Jones made the best doughnuts ever.

Molly sat down on a bench outside the bakery. She took a great big bite out of her doughnut. "Yuk!" she said, spitting it out. It tasted disgusting.

Tiffany and Carlos, two of Molly's school friends, walked by. "You're eating one of Mr Jones's doughnuts, aren't you?" Carlos asked. "They used to be lovely, but not any more. We've stopped buying them."

"I don't blame you," said Molly, throwing the rest of her doughnut in the bin. She heard giggling and turned round. It was John and Jamie, Mr Jones's naughty twin sons.

"What's so funny?" Molly asked crossly.

"Nothing," they said. They ran quickly back into the bakery, still giggling.

"I wonder if the twins are somehow behind the disgusting doughnuts?" said Molly thoughtfully.

"I bet they are!" Tiffany replied. "Do you remember when they watered down all the glue at school so it wouldn't stick?"

"Let's find out!" said Carlos.

The three friends crept into the bakery. John and Jamie were in the kitchen.

"Look what they're doing!" whispered Molly. John and

Jamie were pouring salt into their dad's sugar shaker.

So this was what had happened to Mr Jones's doughnuts! He was sweetening them with salt instead of sugar.

Molly grabbed hold of John and Jamie and dragged them into the shop. John was still holding the sugar shaker. Jamie was pretending to cry.

"Look what John and Jamie have been doing, Mr Jones!" said Molly. "They've been putting salt on your doughnuts and spoiling them."

Mr Jones was very annoyed. "You two can spend the weekend cleaning the kitchen," he said.

Then he turned to Molly, Tiffany and Carlos. "Thank you! You can each take home a free box of cakes," he said, smiling. "But I'll understand if you don't choose doughnuts!"

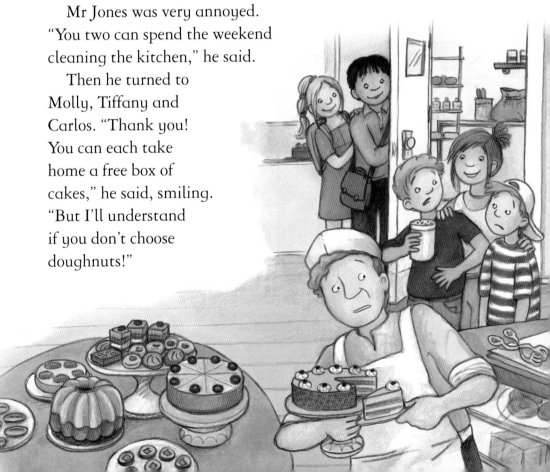

May's Star Surprise

May had lots of ballet posters on her bedroom walls. They all showed her favourite ballet star – Anna Jones.

Anna Jones had learned to dance at the Starlight Ballet School.

"I want to dance like Anna Jones when I grow up," said May to her mum.

"She went to your ballet school," said her mum.

"I know," said May.

A few days later May and her mum and dad arrived at the Starlight Ballet School for May's class.

They arrived at the same time as a lady on her own.

Just as the lady was going into the ballet school she dropped her keys.

The keys dropped into a narrow gap under the doorstep. The lady tried to get them out, but her hands were a little bit too big.

May ran over to help. Her hands were small enough to reach into the gap. She fished out the keys and gave them to the lady.

The lady turned to May. "Thank you," she said.

May gasped.

It was Anna Jones!

"Are you going to your dance class?" said Anna Jones.

May nodded. She couldn't speak.

"Miss Silver asked me to teach your class today," smiled Anna.

"Wow!" said May.

"Look! It's Anna Jones! She's talking to May!" said May's friends.

All the students got dressed quickly.

Anna Jones took the class while Miss Silver sat and watched.

Anna was the most graceful ballerina May had ever seen. May watched Anna closely and tried to move like she did.

"Well done, May!" cried Anna, when May did a beautiful arabesque. "That was lovely."

May had never been able to do an arabesque well before. She couldn't stop smiling as she danced.

"What did you think of the class?" her mum asked at the end of the lesson.

"It was the best class ever!" said May.

Molly Mouse

Kate's mum owned a pet shop. Kate sometimes helped Mum in the shop. She loved helping with the animals.

One Saturday morning a boy from Kate's school called Jim came to buy a mouse. He picked a grey mouse.

"I will call her Molly," said Jim, stroking the mouse. Molly squeaked.

"Hello, Molly," said Kate.

Just then the door opened and a woman came in with a dog. The dog barked loudly when he saw all the other animals in the pet shop.

Molly squeaked and jumped out of Jim's hands.

"Oh, no!" said Kate. "Where are you, Molly?"

They looked under the table. Molly wasn't there.

They looked behind the counter. Molly wasn't there.

They looked under the cash register. Molly wasn't there.

Finally, Kate and Jim looked in the mouse cage. And Molly was there!

"What a sensible mouse!" said Kate's mum.

Molly was happy to see Jim. She ran over to him, squeaking happily.

"And it looks like she already knows who owns her," said Kate.

Tiger

Three kittens were in Kate's mum's pet shop. One kitten was black and white. One kitten was pure white. One kitten was orange and stripy like a tiger. Kate liked the orange kitten best.

A family came into the shop after school one day.

"Which kitten do you want?" the mum said to the little girl.

"I like the black and white kitten best," said the little girl, stroking him. So they took the black and white kitten home.

A few days later a woman came into the shop.

"How cute!" she cried when she saw the white kitten's fluffy fur. So she took the white kitten home.

Days went by. No one picked the orange kitten. Kate played with him. She thought he missed his brother and sister.

Mum watched Kate playing with the kitten.

"Would you like to have that kitten, Kate?" she said.

"Really?" said Kate. She had never had a pet of her own.

"Really," said Mum. Kate laughed. The kitten purred.

"I will call him Tiger," said Kate.

Now the Day Is Over

Now the day is over,
Night is drawing nigh,
Shadows of evening
Steal across the sky.

Now the darkness gathers,
Stars begin to peep,
Birds and beasts and flowers
Soon will be asleep.

I Saw a Ship

I saw a ship a-sailing,
A-sailing on the sea;
And, oh! it was all laden
With pretty things for thee!

There were comfits in the cabin,
And apples in the hold
The sails were made of silk,
And the masts were made of gold.

The four-and-twenty sailors
That stood between the decks,
Were four-and-twenty white mice
With chains about their necks.

The captain was a duck,
With a packet on his back;
And when the ship began to move,
The captain said, "Quack! quack!"

Fairer Princess Sarah

Sarah was the fairest royal princess in the land,
And every prince for miles around longed to win her hand.
But though she was a picture – the loveliest you've seen –
Sarah had another side. She could be *really* mean!

She wouldn't even let her friends touch her things, you see.
"Hands off my pretty toys," she'd shout. "They all belong to me!
Leave my precious jewels alone, and *please* don't touch my dress!
You'll only get it dirty, and make a horrid mess!"

Her friends grew quickly quite fed up: "Just keep your silly stuff.
We don't want to play with you. This time we've had enough!"
"How dare they speak to me like that!"cried Sarah in surprise.
She ran off to the woods to sulk, tears filling up her eyes.

Then Sarah heard a gentle voice. "There is no need to cry!
Every problem can be solved," said thoughtful Sir MacEye.
"Though your eyes shine like stars, and though you may be fair...
A kindly heart means so much more, so why not try to share?"

Sarah listened to his words. "How wise you are," she said.
"I don't need so many things! I'll share them out instead.
For though I love pretty things and clothes that make me fairer,
I'd rather share with my friends, and just be plain old Sarah!"

Where Are You Going to, My Pretty Maid?

Where are you going to, my pretty maid?
Where are you going to, my pretty maid?
I'm going a-milking, sir, she said,
Sir, she said, sir, she said,
I'm going a-milking, sir, she said.

May I go with you, my pretty maid?
May I go with you, my pretty maid?
You're kindly welcome, sir, she said,
Sir, she said, sir, she said,
You're kindly welcome, sir, she said.

What is your fortune, my pretty maid?
What is your fortune, my pretty maid?
My face is my fortune, sir, she said,
Sir, she said, sir, she said,
My face is my fortune, sir, she said.

Then I can't marry you, my pretty maid,
Then I can't marry you, my pretty maid,
Nobody asked you, sir, she said,
Sir, she said, sir, she said,
Nobody asked you, sir, she said.

Monday's Child

Monday's child is fair of face,
Tuesday's child is full of grace,
Wednesday's child is full of woe,
Thursday's child has far to go,
Friday's child is loving and giving,
Saturday's child works hard for his living,
And the child that is born on the Sabbath day
Is bonny and blithe and good and gay.

The Case of the Ghost in the Attic

Molly was doing her homework with Carlos one evening when there was a knock at the front door. It was Mrs Dimley, the next-door neighbour. She looked a bit frightened.

"Is anything the matter?" asked Molly's mum.

"I think my house is haunted!" Mrs Dimley replied.

Molly grew excited. She loved ghost stories.

"At night, I can hear bumping coming from my attic," explained Mrs Dimley.

Molly's mum made everyone a nice cup of tea, and Mrs Dimley said she felt better.

But next evening Mrs Dimley came back looking upset. "My lights aren't working now, and the TV keeps going on and off," she said. "If this doesn't stop, I'll have to move house!"

Molly didn't want her to leave. It was time to investigate!

"Mum, can we borrow a torch?" she asked. "We're going next door to look in Mrs Dimley's attic."

"I'll come with

you," said her dad.

Molly's dad helped her and Carlos up into Mrs Dimley's attic. When Molly switched on her torch, she couldn't believe her eyes. What a mess! There were shredded newspapers everywhere. Hiding in a corner there was a family of frightened squirrels.

"Dad!" called Molly. "Look what we've found!"

Her dad climbed up the ladder and looked into the attic. "Those squirrels must have got in through that hole in the roof," he chuckled. "They've chewed through lots of wires. No wonder Mrs Dimley's electricity isn't working properly!"

Carlos ran next door to tell Mrs Dimley the news.

"Thank goodness for that!" she said. She phoned a vet, who came round straight away.

"I'll take your squirrels to the local park," he said.

"And I'll mend the hole in your roof," said Molly's dad.

Mrs Dimley was pleased. "You're all so kind," she said. She gave Molly and Carlos a big hug. "And you two are very clever kids!"

Star Light, Star Bright

Star light, star bright,
First star I see tonight,
I wish I may, I wish I might,
Have the wish I wish tonight.

Little Cottage

Little cottage in the wood,
Little old man by the window stood,
Saw a rabbit running by,
Knocking at the door.
"Help me! Help me! Help me!" he said,
"Before the huntsman shoots me dead."
"Come little rabbit, come inside,
Safe with me abide."

Here Is the Church

Here is the church,
Here is the steeple,
Open the doors,
And here are the people.
Here is the parson,
Going upstairs,
And here he is
A-saying his prayers.

How Many Miles to Babylon?

How many miles to Babylon? –
Threescore and ten.
Can I get there by candlelight? –
Aye, and back again!

A Swarm of Bees in May

A swarm of bees in May
Is worth a load of hay;
A swarm of bees in June
Is worth a silver spoon;
A swarm of bees in July
Is not worth a fly.

Tinker, Tailor

Tinker, tailor,
Soldier, sailor,
Rich man, poor man,
Beggarman, thief!

Trudie in the Spotlight

It was show night at the Starlight Ballet School, but Trudie had hurt her foot while riding her bike the day before. She wouldn't be able to dance in the show.

On the way to watch the show Trudie's mum tried to cheer her up.

"You'll be in the next show," she said.

"But not this show," said Trudie, with a sniff.

When they got to the Starlight Ballet School Trudie went backstage to wish her friends luck.

"Good luck, Lucy," said Trudie.

Lucy gave Trudie a big hug. "I wish you could be in the show, too," she said.

Just then Miss Silver came into the room. She looked worried. "Has anyone seen the clown doll?" she asked.

"No," said everyone.

"Oh dear!" said Miss Silver. "I think it's lost!"

The clown doll was very important because the dancers danced around it during the big dance at the end of the show.

"We won't be able to do the clown dance," said Lucy.

"The show will be ruined!" cried May.

Trudie looked at all the costumes hanging on the wall. There was an old clown costume hanging there that had been used for a show the previous year.

Trudie had an idea.

"Miss Silver, I could dress up as the clown doll," she said.

"Well done, Trudie!" said Miss Silver. "What a good idea. You have saved the day."

Trudie raced out to tell her parents what had happened and then put on the clown costume.

 At the end of the show all the dancers gathered on stage.

"And we'd like to give special thanks to Trudie for her quick thinking," said Miss Silver. "She really saved the show."

Everyone applauded. Trudie smiled broadly. She had got to be in the show after all!

The Midnight Fairies

Megan was staying with Grandma for a few days, while Mum was away.

Megan always had fun at Grandma's. But on the second night of Megan's visit, as she was getting ready for bed, Megan realized that she'd lost the pretty flower necklace Mum had given her. Megan and Grandma looked everywhere, but they couldn't find it.

Grandma gave Megan a hug. "Don't worry. We'll look in the garden tomorrow," she promised. "I'm sure it will be there."

Megan settled down to sleep, but she tossed and turned and finally woke up again. She couldn't stop thinking about her lost necklace.

Getting out of bed, she went to look out of the window. Somewhere in the distance, a clock chimed once... twice... twelve times. "Midnight!" Megan thought. Suddenly her eyes opened wide. At the bottom of the moonlit garden, where the wild flowers grew, lights began to wink and twinkle, and shimmering shapes danced in the air.

Fairies had come out to play! They danced and skipped through the air, laughing and flitting from flower to flower.

All at once Fairy Firefly spotted something – a silver necklace gleaming in the grass.

"Look!" she said to her fairy friends.

"I wonder who this belongs to!"

"Maybe it's that little girl's," said Nightingale, pointing up to the window where Megan was looking out. "She looks very sad – as if she's lost something special."

"I wish we could make her smile again," said Moon Blossom.

The fairies looked at one another, and knew they were all thinking the same thing. First, they tucked the necklace safely behind a stone. Then, together, they flew across the garden and straight up to Megan's window.

As Megan gasped with amazement and delight, Stardust sprinkled her with glittering fairy dust.

"Now you'll be able to fly with us!" the fairies said happily.

With a fairy holding each hand, Megan whooshed out of the window and flew down to the bottom of the garden. When they landed, Stardust introduced herself and her friends. "We are the Midnight Fairies," she explained. "Every night at midnight, we come out to dance and play in the moonlight.

Will you be our friend and play with us tonight?"

"Of course I will!" said Megan happily.

With the moon beaming down and the friendly stars twinkling above, Megan and the fairies danced among the wild flowers. The cool grass tickled Megan's toes, and the fairies' laughter sounded like tiny crystal bells. Megan laughed with them, and felt happier than she ever had before.

When Megan was too tired to dance any more, Firefly said, "We have a surprise for you." She brought out Megan's necklace.

"My necklace!" cried Megan. "You found it! Thank you!"

As Firefly gave the necklace back, Stardust sprinkled magic fairy dust over it. A beautiful fairy appeared in place of the flower.

"Oh!" breathed Megan. "How wonderful. It's you! It's a Midnight Fairy!"

"Yes," said Firefly. "But please don't tell anyone how it got there, or we might lose our fairy magic."

"I promise!" replied Megan.

As she put on her

necklace, Megan realized that she could barely keep her eyes open. With the Midnight Fairies fluttering over her, she curled up under the oak tree and fell asleep... until the morning, when she woke up, tucked up in her cosy bed in Grandma's house!

"How did I get back here?" Megan wondered. "Was it just a dream?"

She reached up to her neck – and there was her necklace, right where it should be.

"Hello!" said Grandma cheerfully, opening the bedroom door.

"Grandma, look!" said Megan. "I have my necklace back! Did *you* find it?"

"No, dear," said Grandma, with a puzzled look. She peered down at the necklace. "Oh, how lovely!" she said. "I hadn't noticed the fairy before."

"The Midnight Fairies!" Megan thought to herself. "So it wasn't a dream, after all!"

"I wonder how your necklace got back here," said Grandma, scratching her head.

Megan, smiling as she looked out towards the garden, knew the answer. But it was a secret that belonged to her – to her and the Midnight Fairies, the wonderful, magical friends she would never, ever forget.

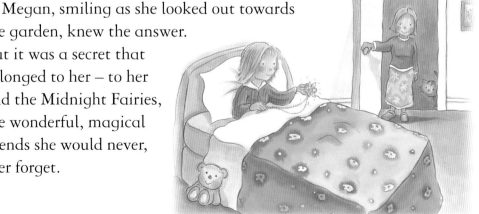

Fudge Won't Play

Sam had a pet hamster. Her name was Fudge.

Sam's sister Sophie wanted to play with Fudge.

"Fudge won't play," said Sam. "She's hiding."

Sophie looked in Fudge's cage. The hamster was curled up inside her nest.

Mum looked at Fudge. "Fudge is getting very plump," she said. "We will take her to the vet."

Sam, Sophie and Mum went in the car to the vet. The vet picked up Fudge and looked at her.

"Is Fudge ill?" said Sam.

The vet smiled. "No," she said, stroking Fudge. "Fudge is going to have babies."

"Can we keep all the babies?" asked Sophie.

"We'll see," said Mum.

Sam put Fudge back in her cage and they went home in the car.

All the way back they talked excitedly about Fudge's babies.

"I wonder how many babies Fudge will have," said Sophie.

"I wonder what colour they will be," said Sam.

"Dad will be surprised, won't he?" said Sophie.

"He certainly will!" said Mum.

Sam held Fudge's cage carefully all the way home. But the three of them were so busy talking about Fudge's babies that they didn't notice the door of the cage wasn't closed properly.

At home Dad went to look at Fudge. He came back with a frown on his face.

"Fudge isn't in her cage," said Dad.

Sam and Sophie raced upstairs. The cage door was open.

"Fudge is missing!" said Sam.

"What will happen to her babies?" said Sophie.

"Don't panic," said Mum. "I'm sure we'll find her. Sophie, you look upstairs. Sam, you go and look in the car."

Sam ran out to look in the car. A minute later he came racing back in with a big smile on his face. "I found her," he said. "And there's a surprise in the car, too!"

They went to look in the car.

"Here she is!" said Sam.

Fudge was on the back seat. And so were all her babies!

Lost Billy

Kate and her mum were walking in the park when a dog started to follow them.

"Woof!" barked the dog mournfully. Kate looked at him.

"He looks lost," she said.

Mum bent down to pat him. "He does," she agreed. "But he doesn't have a collar so we don't know who he belongs to."

Kate's mum took the dog back to her pet shop. She put a card in the window saying that they had found a brown and white dog with black ears and a black tail.

A few days later a boy came into the pet shop. As soon as he walked through the door the dog started barking excitedly. He jumped up and started licking the boy's face.

"Billy!" said the boy, with a big smile on his face.

"Woof!" barked Billy happily, jumping all around Jamal.

"My name's Jamal," said the boy. "Billy is my dog."

Jamal put a new collar on Billy. "Now Billy won't get lost," he said.

Kate was sad. "I will miss Billy," she said.

"Come and play with us whenever you want," said Jamal.

"OK!" said Kate, smiling. She had two new friends!

Pretty Polly

It was Mum's birthday. Kate wanted to get her a present.

"What do you think I should get Mum?" she asked Jamal.

"Maybe a bag," said Jamal.

"Maybe a bag," squawked Polly Parrot.

Kate shook her head.

"Maybe a mug," said Jamal.

"Maybe a mug," said Polly.

Kate shook her head.

"Maybe a hat," said Jamal.

"Maybe a hat," said Polly.

"Good idea!" said Kate.

Kate and Jamal and Jamal's mum went to the hat shop. They picked out a hat for Mum. They wrapped it in paper and tied it with a ribbon.

Kate gave Mum the present.

"I wonder what it is?" Mum said.

"Maybe a bag," squawked Polly Parrot.

"Shhh, Polly," said Kate. Mum took off the ribbon.

"Maybe a mug," said Polly.

"Shhh, Polly," said Kate. Mum took off the paper.

"Maybe a hat!" said Polly.

"What a pretty hat," said Mum.

"What a pretty hat," squawked Polly.

Here We Go Round the Mulberry Bush

Here we go round the mulberry bush,
The mulberry bush, the mulberry bush,
Here we go round the mulberry bush,
On a cold and frosty morning.

This is the way we wash our hands,
Wash our hands, wash our hands,
This is the way we wash our hands,
On a cold and frosty morning.

This is the way we wash our clothes,
Wash our clothes, wash our clothes,
This is the way we wash our clothes,
On a cold and frosty morning.

Here we go round the mulberry bush,
The mulberry bush, the mulberry bush,
Here we go round the mulberry bush,
On a cold and frosty morning.

Lavender's Blue

Lavender's blue,
Dilly, dilly,
Lavender's green,
When I am king,
Dilly, dilly,
You shall be queen.

Call up your men,
Dilly, dilly,
Set them to work,
Some to the plough,
Dilly, dilly,
Some to the cart;

Some to make hay,
Dilly, dilly,
Some to thresh corn;
Whilst you and I,
Dilly, dilly,
Keep ourselves warm.

245

Incey Wincey Spider

Incey Wincey spider
Climbing up the spout;
Down came the rain
And washed the spider out.
Out came the sunshine
And dried up all the rain;
Incey Wincey spider
Climbing up again.

Bow, Wow, Wow

Bow, wow, wow,
Whose dog art thou?
"Little Tom Tinker's dog,
Bow, wow, wow."

The Cold Old House

I know a house, and a cold old house,
A cold old house by the sea.
If I were a mouse in that cold old house
What a cold, cold mouse I'd be!

Hickory, Dickory, Dock

Hickory, dickory, dock,
The mouse ran up the clock.
The clock struck one,
The mouse ran down,
Hickory, dickory, dock.

Bat, Bat

Bat, bat, come under my hat,
And I'll give you a slice of bacon,
And when I bake I'll give you a cake,
If I am not mistaken.

Little Jack Horner

Little Jack Horner,
Sat in a corner,
Eating a Christmas pie.
He put in his thumb,
And pulled out a plum,
And said, "What a good boy am I!"

Twinkle the Tooth Fairy

Twinkle the Tooth Fairy was always very busy. Every night, she collected the milk teeth that the children left under their pillows. But the teeth were so tiny they were difficult to find in the dark.

Late one summer's evening, Twinkle was looking for the last milk tooth of the night. Finally she found it and put her last shiny coin under the pillow.

"Goodnight," whispered Twinkle as she gently kissed the sleeping child and flew silently out of the window. The sun was just coming up as Twinkle flew back to Fairyland.

All the fairies in Fairyland were very busy getting ready for the Fairy Ball. Fairy food had to be made by the best fairy cooks. Hundreds of fairy lights had to be put up. And the fairy orchestra was practising very hard.

Before going to bed, Twinkle decided to go and see her friend Thimble, the fairy dressmaker. Thimble had been busy too, making all the dresses for the Fairy Ball.

"What beautiful dresses!" exclaimed Twinkle.

"I'm glad you like them," said Thimble. "But they would be so much better if I could decorate them with golden thread. I can't find any in the whole of Fairyland."

"I know where there's lots of golden thread. Leave it to me," Twinkle said excitedly, and she flew off high into the sky.

Soon, she was among hundreds of bright, shining stars. On she flew, until she reached a huge golden ball – the Sun.

"Please, Mr Sun," she asked, "can you spare some of your fine golden thread for my friend Thimble?"

Twinkle waited. All of a sudden, a long trail of golden thread came slowly from the centre of the Sun. Twinkle took the end of it, and began to pull it towards her.

"That tickles!" laughed the Sun.

Twinkle had soon gathered a large bundle of the precious thread. "Thank you, Mr Sun," she said.

"You're very welcome, Twinkle," chuckled the Sun.

When Thimble saw what Twinkle had brought her, she clapped her hands with joy!

"Thank you, Twinkle!" she said. "Now my dresses will be perfect. And I promise you will have the finest dress of all for the ball."

"I've never been to the Fairy Ball," said Twinkle quietly.

"Why ever not?" asked Thimble, curiously.

"It takes me such a long time to

find all the children's teeth, I never get back in time," Twinkle said sadly.

"Don't you worry. I'll think of something!" said Thimble.

Twinkle felt very tired after her busy night and went straight to bed. When she woke up the next day, she was surprised to see a large bag at the foot of her bed.

Inside the bag were the most beautiful purple and gold velvet purses. Pinned to the bag was a note, which read:

Dear Twinkle,

I have made these special purses from the left-over fairy dress cloth. The children can put their teeth into them. The purses will be much easier for you to find in the dark. With a bit of luck, you will be back in time for the ball!

Your best fairy friend, Thimble

Later that evening, Twinkle collected all the children's milk

teeth as usual. She left each child with a shiny coin tucked into one of the purses, which she carefully placed under their pillows. Twinkle whispered to each sleeping child, "Please use the purse to keep your next milk tooth safe."

A few days later it was the night of the Fairy Ball. Twinkle was very excited. She so hoped that she'd be back in time to join in the fun! But first she had her important job to do.

When she flew off that night to collect the milk teeth, Twinkle was overjoyed to see that each child had put their milk tooth inside their purse. Now, they were easy to find!

She kissed each child and whispered, "Thank you!"

After gathering all the teeth up carefully, Twinkle flew quickly back to Fairyland. When she was nearly home, she

could hear the sounds of the fairy orchestra in the distance. The whole sky was lit up with the lights of the Fairy Ball.

"It's already started!" she thought, flying even faster.

When she reached home, Twinkle rushed to see Thimble.

"Am I too late?" she asked breathlessly.

"It's only just begun!" laughed Thimble.

Twinkle had a wonderful time at the Fairy Ball. And everyone agreed that in her beautiful new dress, she was the prettiest fairy of all.

Rain, Rain, Go Away!

It was a rainy day and Raindrop the fairy liked the rain.

"Come and play outside," Raindrop said to the other fairies.

The other fairies did not like the rain. "It's too wet to play outside," they said.

All the fairies lived at the bottom of a garden that belonged to Ann and Tom.

Ann and Tom looked out of the window.

"I'm bored," said Ann.

"It's too wet to play outside," said Tom.

"I'm bored of being inside," said Ann.

Down at the bottom of the garden, Raindrop had started to cry because no one wanted to play with her. And the more Raindrop cried, the more it rained. Soon it was pouring!

Sunny the sunshine fairy looked at the rain. "Don't cry, Raindrop," she said. "I will play with you."

Raindrop stopped crying. Like magic, the rain stopped. The sun came out.

Ann and Tom came out to play in the garden.

"Look! A beautiful rainbow!" they said.

Too Much Sun

It was a hot sunny day. Tom and Ann were too hot to play. They lay on the sofa and watched TV. Even the flowers in the garden were wilting in the hot sun.

"It's just too hot!" said Ann.

But Sunny the sunshine fairy, down at the bottom of Ann and Tom's garden, liked the sun. The hotter the better!

"Come and play in the sky," she said to her fairy friends.

Sunny, Windy and Raindrop flew up into the sky. The fairies started to play hide-and-seek.

First of all Sunny hid in the clouds. Then Windy blew the clouds away.

Then Raindrop waved her wand at a cloud and it began to rain. She hid in the shower of rain until Windy blew the raincloud away with a laugh.

The flowers in Ann and Tom's garden lifted up their petals gratefully when the refreshing shower of rain came down.

Now it was not too hot any more. It was a lovely day and everything was sparkling from the shower of rain.

Tom and Ann were not too hot any more.

"Let's go and play in the garden!" said Tom.

The Case of the Stolen Necklace

"Happy birthday, Tiffany!" Molly said, hugging her friend.

The birthday party began with a magic show in the garden. Everyone was amazed at the magician's clever tricks.

But then suddenly, Tiffany's mum, Tracy, ran onto the stage. "Stop the show!" she cried. "I can't find my necklace!"

"Your diamond necklace?" asked Tiffany's dad worriedly.

"Yes – and it's worth a fortune!" said Tiffany's mum.

"Mummy's always losing her jewels and panicking," said Tiffany crossly. "I bet it's not stolen at all. And it's ruined my birthday party!"

Molly wanted to help Tiffany.

"I might just, er, go to the toilet, Tiff," she said.

On the way up to the house, Molly heard a scream behind a hedge.

Behind the hedge she found Tiffany's two little sisters in their Wendy house. They were dressed as princesses.

"It's mine! Give it back!" said Zara.

"No, I got it first!" said Trixie. She was waving a sparkly necklace.

"Hello, you two," said Molly. "Where did you get that lovely necklace?"

"We borrowed it," said Trixie.

Molly laughed. "I think we'd better tell your mum," she said.

Tiffany's mum was very happy to have her necklace back. "Next time, just ask before you borrow my things," she said, giving Zara and Trixie a hug. "Now let's find Tiffany and get this magic show started again!"

After the magic show was over, Tiffany's mum made another announcement. "Good news!" she cried. "My necklace has been found. And to celebrate, all the girls are invited to try on my jewellery collection."

Tiffany clapped excitedly. "Come on everyone!" she cried. "This is going to be the best birthday ever!"

Poor Peep

Sophie and Sam were playing in the garden when Miss Tring from next door came out of her house. "Peep!" she called. "Peep! Where are you?"

Peep was Miss Tring's cat.

"Is Peep missing, Miss Tring?" asked Sophie.

"Yes," said Miss Tring. "She's been missing since last night. I can't find her."

"We'll help you look for her," said Sam.

Sam and Sophie began to look. They looked all over their garden. Then Sophie heard a noise.

"What's that noise?" she said. "Where's it coming from?"

"Listen!" said Sam. The noise was coming from a big metal bin Sophie and Sam's dad sometimes used to keep garden rubbish in.

"Miaow! Miaow!" Sam ran to the bin and opened the lid. Peep was inside. She miaowed even louder.

They lifted Peep out and took her home to Miss Tring.

"She must have climbed in yesterday when Dad was working in the garden," said

Sophie to Miss Tring.

"I'm just glad she's home again," said Miss Tring.

"Miaow!" miaowed Peep, lifting up one of her front paws.

"Poor Peep! She has cut her paw!" said Sophie.

"We'll need to take her to the vet," said Miss Tring. "Would you like to come with me?"

"Yes, please!" said Sophie and Sam.

The vet stroked Peep. "Nothing serious, Peep," she said. "You'll soon be better." She cleaned Peep's paw and put a bandage on it.

"All better now, Peep!" said Sam, stroking her gently.

Peep began to purr.

Miss Tring smiled. "Thank you for helping!" she said.

Fairy Seasons

Spring fairies laugh and play,
Hopping and skipping
With bunnies all day.
Hop, skip, hop, skip,
To make the garden happy.
Summer fairies flutter around,
Cleaning and shining
The flowers on the ground.
Softly, softly, clean and shine,
To make the garden pretty.
Autumn fairies dance round the trees,
Catching and chasing

The leaves in the breeze.
Hurry, scurry, catch the leaves,
To make the garden tidy.
Winter fairies float through the air,
Sprinkling and shaking
Snow here and there.
Gently, gently, spread the snow,
To make the garden sparkle.
Then, once a year, as a special treat,
The fairy queen and the fairies meet.
They sing and dance to celebrate
The magic in the garden.

My Mum Is Great

My mum is great.

She's brilliant at everything. I think my mum's... *magic*!

Every morning, her magic begins when she disappears into the bathroom. She changes from morning Mummy... into daytime Mummy! After that, Mum is ready to tackle anything

– even the horrible monsters that live under my bed.

Isn't my mum brave?

My mum's not afraid of anything. I'm never worried when she's around.

My mum never lets me down. She even manages to find Little Ted after I've looked everywhere – and given up hope of ever seeing him again.

Then, for her next trick, Mum mends my Mr Wobbly.

You would never know he'd been broken.

In fact, my mum can fix

just about anything (except washing machines).

My mum always knows when I've done something wrong.

But she never stays cross with me for long.

Mum and I always have fun. Sometimes she takes me for bike rides in the country.

My mum is ever so smart. She always knows the answers to my questions.

And she's a fantastic cook. She makes me the yummiest meals.

My mum makes me smile when I'm sad. And she can always make me feel better with a magical hug.

Towards the end of the day Mum's magic begins to fade. By the time I'm ready for bed she has changed back into morning Mummy.

But I don't care what Mum looks like. I don't even care if she's not really magic, because whatever she does, she's my mum and... my mum is *great*!

Jolly Princess Polly

Polly was a funny kind of princess, it was thought.
She didn't always act the way a royal princess ought.
For everywhere that Polly went and every time she spoke,
She really couldn't help herself – *out* would pop a joke!

She sniggered at royal functions, and laughed aloud at school.
She giggled in the library and broke the silence rule!
But though Polly was great fun, and made her best friends smile,
She did get quite annoying – laughing all the while!

"If only Polly made less noise, and played more quietly,
Instead of laughing fit to burst!" complained her family.
Then one day disaster struck. Poor Polly lost her kitty.
She couldn't even raise a smile! It really was a pity.

"I wish you would laugh once more," her friends said, that night.
"Without your laughter and your jokes, the palace isn't right!
If only we could find poor Fluff and make you smile again.
If we lose your happy face, it just won't be the same!"

All at once Sir Dave appeared, in answer to their wish.
"I found this by the moat," he said, "watching all the fish!"
Princess Polly laughed out loud, to everyone's delight.
"You've found little Fluff!" she cried, kissing the blushing knight.

Now Polly's jolly once again, so if they're feeling sad,
Her friends just listen to her laugh. It always makes them glad!

Polly Put the Kettle On

Polly put the kettle on,
Polly put the kettle on,
Polly put the kettle on,
We'll all have tea.

Sukey take it off again,
Sukey take it off again,
Sukey take it off again,
They've all gone away.

I Scream

I scream, you scream,
We all scream for ice cream!

A Peanut

A peanut sat on the railway track,
His heart was all a-flutter;
Along came a train – the 9:15 –
Toot, toot, peanut butter!

Our Baby

Goodness, our baby makes a lot of noise!
He bangs his cot and throws out all his toys.
But there's one time I love to take a peep,
And that's when, finally, he falls asleep.

Pat-a-Cake

Pat-a-cake, pat-a-cake, baker's man,
Bake me a cake as fast as you can.
Pat it and prick it and mark it with B,
And put it in the oven for Baby and me.

Dibbity, Dibbity, Dibbity, Doe

Dibbity, dibbity, dibbity, doe,
Give me a pancake
And I'll go.
Dibbity, dibbity, dibbity, ditter,
Please to give me
A bit of a fritter.

Like a Duck to Water

Mrs Duck swam proudly across the farm pond followed by a line of fluffy ducklings. Hidden in the safety of the nest, Dozy Duckling peeked out and watched them go. He wished he was brave enough to go with them but he was afraid of the water!

When they returned that night they told him tales of all the scary animals they had met by the pond.

"There's a big thing with hot breath called Horse," said Dotty.

"There's a huge smelly pink thing called Pig," said Dickie.

"But worst of all," said Doris, "there's a great grey bird called Heron. He gobbles up little ducklings for breakfast!"

At that all the little ducklings squawked with fear and excitement.

Next morning, Mrs Duck hurried the ducklings out for their morning parade. Dozy kept his eyes shut until they had gone, then looked up to see a great grey bird towering over him! He leaped into the water crying, "Help, wait for me!" But the others started laughing!

"It's a trick! Heron won't eat you. We just wanted you to come swimming. And you've taken to it like a duck to water!"

Maud and the Monster

Maud thought she was very brave. All the things which frightened other children were her favourites – slimy eggs, spider's legs and even the dark.

One day, as Maud walked past the cellar door, she noticed that the light was on. Without a second thought, she dashed down the stairs. But, as Maud reached the bottom step, she heard the cellar door bang shut – which turned the light off!

"I'm not scared!" said Maud, defiantly. Then she noticed a strange humming sound. She crept forwards, feeling along the wall, and peered slowly into the darkness. Round the corner was a bright, white monstrous shape! Maud screamed!

The cellar door burst open and the light came on. Maud's mum came rushing down.

"Help, Mum! There's a monster!" cried Maud – but then, as they both looked at where she was pointing, Maud realized it was the freezer!

Maud felt rather silly. After that she didn't boast about her bravery any more – well, not much!

Windy's Blowy Day

Windy the fairy was fast asleep on an orange flower.

Because Windy was fast asleep there was no wind. The leaves hung still on the trees. Tom and Ann's dad's washing did not dry. He looked out of the window and sighed.

"We need some wind, kids," he said. "Or your school clothes won't be dry by tomorrow morning."

Tom and Ann went to the bottom of the garden to play with their new kite. Tom held the strings and Ann lifted the kite up, but when she let go the kite just fell to the ground.

"The kite won't fly," said Tom.

"It won't fly because there's no wind," sighed Ann.

Their voices woke Windy up. She saw the kite.

"That looks fun," she said to herself. Windy wanted to play with the kite.

Windy blew. Suddenly the kite lifted out of Ann's hands. Windy blew some more. The kite flew into the air.

"The kite's flying!" cried Tom. The kite flew high into the sky. Windy flew after it! She flitted around the kite laughing merrily.

And the washing blew dry on the line ready for school on Monday!

Christmas Tree Fairy

It was Christmas Eve and Carly and Jordan were too excited to sleep.

"Are you still awake?" whispered Carly.

"Yes," whispered Jordan.

"Mum and Dad are asleep," whispered Carly. "Let's go downstairs and see if we can surprise Father Christmas!"

Carly and Jordan crept downstairs and peeped through the door of the living room. Everything was dark except the Christmas tree, whose lights were still twinkling.

Carly gasped. "Look!" she said. The fairy on top of the Christmas tree had come to life. She was waving her wand over the presents under the tree. Every time she waved the wand, a new present appeared.

Carly and Jordan watched until the fairy had finished her work, then they crept back upstairs.

The next day when they opened the presents under the tree, Mum looked a bit puzzled.

"The label says they're from me, but I don't remember buying those," she said, looking at two scarves Carly and Jordan had just opened.

"It must be magic," said Carly, smiling.

"Christmas magic," added Jordan, looking at the fairy on top of the Christmas tree.

The Magical Locket

It was Princess Crystal's birthday.
Her father, the king, had given
Princess Crystal a very special
present – a beautiful locket.

"This is a magical locket," the
king told Princess Crystal. "But, it
will only work if you say the magic
rhyme:

Magical locket, please listen well,
Help my friend with a kindly spell."

No one knew that, far away in
her tower, the wicked witch was watching Princess Crystal's
birthday in her crystal ball. When she saw the locket, the
witch wanted it for herself.

The next day, Princess Crystal went riding
on her favourite horse. She didn't see the
witch hiding behind a tree. As Princess
Crystal trotted by, the wicked witch
cast her evil spell:

"Frogs and toads, and all things black,
Throw the princess on her back!"

Princess Crystal's horse reared up
and threw her to the ground.

As quick as a flash, the wicked witch
took the locket from around Princess

Crystal's neck and threw a net over her.

"Now the locket's mine!" she cackled. She bundled the frightened princess over her shoulder and carried her away.

Soon they arrived at the witch's tower. A fierce dragon guarded it.

"Don't try to escape, my pretty one," said the witch, "or Horace the dragon will eat you up!"

At the top of the tower, the witch freed Princess Crystal.

"Recognize this?" she asked, holding up the magical locket.

"My locket!" gasped Princess Crystal.

"Yes," hissed the witch. "It's mine now. But I need the magic rhyme to go with it."

"I won't give it to you," said Princess Crystal bravely.

"Then you can stay here until you do!" shouted the witch. "Here's your precious locket," she added, throwing it at Princess Crystal. "It won't do you any good locked in here!"

She stormed out of the room, locking the door behind her.

Princess Crystal felt so alone. She leaned out of the window and began to cry. Her tears fell on Horace the dragon below.

"You're making me all wet," he said grumpily, flying up to the window. "I'm not crying, even though my wing's broken, and really hurts."

"Oh, you poor thing," said Princess Crystal, feeling sorry for the dragon. "Maybe I can help you." She closed her eyes, held the locket and said the magic rhyme:

"Magical locket, please listen well,
Help my friend with a kindly spell."

Princess Crystal opened her eyes, and saw that Horace's wing had completely healed.

"Oh, thank you," he said happily. "My wing is healed, and I don't feel grumpy any more. But what can I do to return your kindness?"

"Fly and find Prince Robert as quickly as you can," she said. Horace promised he'd go quickly, and beating his wings he rose into the air. Soon, Horace found Prince Robert. When he heard that Princess Crystal had been captured by the witch, he jumped onto Horace's back and flew to the rescue.

"Thank goodness Horace found you," cried Princess Crystal, as Prince Robert climbed in through the window. But before they could escape, the door suddenly opened.

There stood the wicked witch.

"How nice of you to join us, young man," she cackled. "And how handsome you are! But I think you'd look much better as a... *frog*!"

She began to cast an evil spell.

"Oh, no," thought Princess Crystal. "I'd better do something quickly."

She closed her eyes, held the locket and whispered the magic rhyme:

"Magical locket, please listen well,
Help my friend with a kindly spell."

When Princess Crystal opened her eyes, the locket's magic had worked. The witch's spell had backfired, and turned her into a frog instead!

"Well done, Princess Crystal!" said Prince Robert.

"Frogspawn and slime!" croaked the frog, then hopped out of the window and was never seen again.

And Princess Crystal, Prince Robert and Horace the dragon lived happily ever after.

Sophie's Baby

Sophie was feeling left out.

Sam was feeding his baby hamsters.

Mum was feeding baby Jake.

"What can I do?" thought Sophie.

Just then, the doorbell rang. Sophie opened the door.

"Hello, Sophie!" said the lady at the door. It was the vet.
She was visiting Miss Tring next door.

"Peep has had some kittens," said the vet. "Come and see."

In Miss Tring's house there were four kittens in a box. Three
kittens were grey like Peep. One was small and white.

"What's the white kitten's name?" asked
Sophie.

"His name is Snowy," said Miss Tring.

Snowy was sitting in a corner of the
box.

The vet looked at each kitten
carefully. The three grey kittens
were sucking milk from Peep's
tummy, but Snowy was sitting
on his own. He wasn't sucking
milk from Peep's tummy.

"Snowy needs help to feed,"
said the vet.

She opened her bag and took
out a special bottle. Then she

274

mixed up some warm milk in the bottle.

"Can I help feed Snowy?" asked Sophie.

"Of course," said the vet. "I'll show you what to do."

The vet put a towel on Sophie's lap and put the white kitten on it and put the bottle in Snowy's mouth.

He began to suck! Very gently, Sophie stroked Snowy with a single finger. He was so small that she didn't need to use any more.

Snowy closed his eyes.

He began to purr.

"Now I have a baby to feed," said Sophie.

Ring-a-Ring o' Roses

Ring-a-ring o' roses,
A pocket full of posies,
A-tishoo! A-tishoo!
We all fall down!

See a Pin and Pick It Up

See a pin and pick it up,
All the day you'll have good luck;
See a pin and let it lay,
Bad luck you'll have all the day!

Miss Mary Mack

Miss Mary Mack, Mack, Mack,
All dressed in black, black, black,
With silver buttons, buttons, buttons,
All down her back, back, back.
She went upstairs to make her bed,
She made a mistake and bumped her head;
She went downstairs to wash the dishes,
She made a mistake and washed her wishes;
She went outside to hang her clothes,
She made a mistake and hung her nose.

Mr Nobody

Mr Nobody is a nice young man,
He comes to the door with his hat in his hand.
Down she comes, all dressed in silk,
A rose in her bosom, as white as milk.
She takes off her gloves, she shows me her ring,
Tomorrow, tomorrow, the wedding begins.

Little Sally Waters

Little Sally Waters,
Sitting in the sun,
Crying and weeping,
For a young man.
Rise, Sally, rise,
Dry your weeping eyes,
Fly to the east,
Fly to the west,
Fly to the one you love the best.

Georgie Porgie

Georgie Porgie, pudding and pie,
Kissed the girls and made them cry;
When the boys came out to play
Georgie Porgie ran away.

Minnie and Winnie

Minnie and Winnie
Slept in a shell.
Sleep, little ladies!
And they slept well.

Pink was the shell within,
Silver without;
Sounds of the great sea
Wandered about.

Sleep, little ladies,
Wake not soon!
Echo on echo
Dies to the moon.

Two bright stars
Peeped into the shell.
"What are they dreaming of?
Who can tell?"

Started a green linnet
Out of the croft;
Wake, little ladies,
The sun is aloft!

Lady Moon

Lady Moon, Lady Moon,
Where are you roving?
Over the sea.
Lady Moon, Lady Moon,
Whom are you loving?
All that love me.
Are you not tired with
Rolling, and never
Resting to sleep?
Why look so pale,
And so sad, as for ever
Wishing to weep?

The Case of the Crop Circles

Molly's dad was reading the newspaper. "Look at this!" he said, showing Molly a photo of some huge circles of flattened corn in Farmer Gilbert's cornfield.

"How did they get there?" asked Molly.

"No one knows, but some people say they were made by aliens," her dad replied, with a grin. "Perhaps a UFO landed on the cornfield one night!"

Molly couldn't stop thinking about the crop circles. She didn't believe they were made by aliens. It was a mystery, and she wanted to solve it.

By teatime, she had come up with a plan. "Carlos and I

have to do a bat watch project," she told her dad. "Would you come out with us one night to count bats? I thought we could go to Farmer Gilbert's cornfield."

Her dad smiled. "OK," he agreed. "As there's no school tomorrow, we'll go tonight."

They took a flask of hot cocoa with them up to the cornfield. The moon was shining brightly.

After a couple of hours of counting bats Molly began to feel tired. Her dad gave a loud snore beside her. Molly's own eyes began to close – and then she opened them wide again as she saw something move in the corn. She had almost missed it! Two teenage boys were creeping into the field.

Molly nudged her dad and Carlos. "Look!" she said. The boys started beating down the corn with their skateboards. They moved quickly to make a big circle.

Molly, Carlos and her dad walked over to them. "You can stop that right now!" her dad said.

The boys looked embarrassed. "We were only having a bit of fun," the boys replied. "We like reading about our crop circles in the newspaper."

"If you promise you won't do this again, we won't tell on you," Molly said.

"It's a deal," the boys said, looking relieved.

Next week, Molly ran to the local shop to buy the newspaper as soon as it came out.

"Look, Dad!" Molly showed him the latest photo of Farmer Gilbert's field. "No more crop circles. It says the aliens have left!"

Her dad smiled. "But we know better, don't we?" he said.

Creatures

Here is the ostrich straight and tall,
Nodding his head above us all.
Here is the hedgehog prickly and small,
Rolling himself into a ball.
Here is the spider scuttling around,
Treading so lightly on the ground.
Here are the birds that fly so high,
Spreading their wings across the sky.
Here are the children fast asleep,
And in the night the owls do peep,
Tuit tuwhoo, tuit tuwhoo!

Queen of the Monsters

When the year is quite old, or so I am told,
The monsters all like to convene.
They meet in a cave and they all misbehave,
Casting votes for a new king or queen.

Little Mog went along to join in the throng,
Would she be the one that they'd choose?
She was quite small and sweet, with her four dainty feet,
So the chances were high she would lose.

Hagar the Hairy was terribly scary,
He'd not been around for some time.
With terrible claws on the ends of his paws,
His mouth dribbled poisonous slime.

Most monstrous of all was Slod the Slimeball,
Her warts were a perfect disgrace.
Her favourite ruse was to let out an ooze,
So you'd slip up all over the place.

The monsters agreed, as they sat down to feed,
That Slod was the one they'd all dread.
But who'd want a fiend for a monstrous queen?
So they all voted Mog in instead.

The Little Turtle Dove

High in the pine tree,
The little turtle dove
Made a little nursery
To please her little love.

"Coo," said the turtle dove,
"Coo," said she;
In the long, shady branches
Of the dark pine tree.

Hey, My Kitten

Hey, my kitten, my kitten,
And hey my kitten, my deary,
Such a sweet pet as this
There is not far nor neary.
Here we go up, up, up,
Here we go down, down, downy;
Here we go backwards and forwards,
And here we go round, round, roundy.

Dickery, Dickery, Dare

Dickery, dickery, dare,
The pig flew up in the air.
The man in brown
Soon brought him down!
Dickery, dickery, dare.

Clap Hands

Clap hands, Daddy's coming up the waggon way,
His pockets full of money, and his hands full of clay.

Pussycat Ate the Dumplings

Pussycat ate the dumplings,
Pussycat ate the dumplings,
Mamma stood by,
And cried, "Oh fie!
Why did you eat the dumplings?"

Mrs White

Mrs White had a fright
In the middle of the night.
She saw a ghost, eating toast,
Halfway up a lamp post.

Lucky Digger

One day, Dad met Sophie and Sam after school.

There was a brown and white dog sitting at the school gate.

"Can we pat him?" asked Sophie.

Dad looked at the dog. The dog wagged his tail. "He seems friendly enough," Dad said. "Pat him gently."

Sophie and Sam patted the dog. Then Sophie noticed that he was holding up one paw and limping.

"The dog has hurt his paw!" said Sophie.

"He doesn't have a collar," said Dad. "Maybe he's a stray."

"If he's a stray, who will look after his paw?" asked Sam.

"We will," said Dad. "We will take him to the vet."

The vet cleaned the dog's paw and put a bandage on it.

"Because he doesn't have a collar he will have to go to the dogs' home," she said.

Sophie and Sam and Dad took the dog to the dogs' home.

"What shall we call him?" said the lady at the dogs' home.

"Digger," said Sam and Sophie. Digger wagged his tail.

"What will happen to him now?" asked Sophie.

"He'll live at the dogs' home until a family come along who can give him a new home," said the lady.

"I wish Digger was our dog," said Sam a few days later.

"Can we go and see if Digger is alright?" Sophie asked Mum. "There were lots of big dogs at the dogs' home. They might be bullying Digger."

The next day Mum and Dad took Sophie and Sam to the dogs' home to see Digger.

"Digger is a lucky dog," said the lady. "He has a new home."

"His new family are lucky, too," said Sophie.

"Who is Digger's new family?" said Sam.

"Well... we are!" said Mum. "We've been thinking about getting a dog for a while, and Dad and I decided last night that Digger is just perfect."

"Wow!" said Sophie and Sam.

"Woof!" said Digger, wagging his tail.

The lady smiled. "I think Digger likes you," she said.

"Are you ready to come home with us, Digger?" asked Dad.

Sam and Sophie were happy.

They patted Digger.

Digger barked again. He was happy too!

Magical Shoes

Lily the ballerina was hurrying to the theatre.
Today was the day of the grand ballet. Lily
was dancing with her friends Wanda,
Amber and Tilly. They were all looking
forward to dancing with Fleur.

Fleur was the Prima Ballerina. She
always danced in a magical pair
of silver ballet shoes. Only the Prima
Ballerina could wear them. They would
not work if anyone
else wore them.

The four friends
watched Fleur during the first dance as
she performed a perfect plié, a beautiful
arabesque and a stunning pirouette.
They all loved dancing with Fleur.

After the first dance, everyone hurried
to change their costumes for the next
dance. Suddenly, Fleur appeared in her
bare feet, looking upset.

"Something terrible has happened!"
Fleur exclaimed. "I took off my silver ballet shoes for a moment
and now they have gone. I won't be able to dance until they
are found."

"Don't worry," said Lily kindly. "We'll find them for you."

"We'll find the shoes in time for the next dance," Wanda promised.

The four friends ran outside. As Lily wondered which way she should go, she spotted a magpie flying towards the woods. She could see something silver in its beak.

"The silver shoes!" gasped Lily. "The magpie must have stolen them!"

Lily ran after the magpie as fast as she could. But meanwhile, the ballet shoes grew too heavy for the magpie. They fell from its beak.

The shoes dropped right in front of Wanda, who was searching the woods.

"The magical shoes!" she said. "How beautiful they are. I'll just try them on quickly."

But as soon as Wanda put on the magical shoes a strange thing happened. She suddenly danced a plié. She pliéd up and down and up and down, until she realized she couldn't stop.

Wanda pliéd out of the woods and into the meadow. Soon her legs were so tired she couldn't dance any more. She fell

flat on her back into a nearby bush.

"Are you all right?" asked Amber, who had been searching the meadow.

"Yes thanks," puffed Wanda. "But help me take the shoes off."

Amber pulled off the magical ballet shoes and gazed at them. "They're so beautiful," she said. "I'm sure no one would mind if I tried them on quickly."

Amber tried on the magical shoes and danced a perfect arabesque. "I never knew I could arabesque so well!" she thought. Then she did another, and another, until she realized that she couldn't stop.

"Help! I can't stop!" poor Amber called, as she danced out of the meadow and into the garden. She was so dizzy from dancing that she ended up in the fountain with a big splash.

Luckily, Tilly was nearby and ran to help. But when she saw the silver shoes lying on the ground, she just couldn't resist putting them on.

"They're so beautiful," she said. "I'm sure no one would mind if I tried them on quickly."

But when Tilly tried on the magical shoes a strange thing happened. She started to pirouette around and around...

"Wheee... this is fun!" exclaimed Tilly. "I never knew I could pirouette so well!"

But then she began to spin faster and faster, and realized that she couldn't stop.

Poor Tilly pirouetted down the hill straight into a muddy puddle.

The others caught up with her and helped her up.

Lily carefully took the precious ballet shoes off Tilly's feet.

"They are so beautiful," said Lily, and she wanted to try them on too. But in her heart, she knew that there was only one person who was meant to wear them.

"Let's return the shoes to the Prima Ballerina," Lily said to the others. "She'll be so happy we found them."

"My shoes!" exclaimed Fleur when Lily and the others returned. "Thank you! Now we must get on with the show!"

But Wanda, Amber and Tilly were in such a mess they couldn't go back on stage.

"Oh, dear!" Fleur sighed. "You won't be able to dance looking like that." Then Fleur turned to Lily with a smile. "We will have to dance together."

Lily danced alone with the Prima Ballerina. And they danced so beautifully together that everyone clapped and cheered more than ever.

"I'll remember this evening for ever and ever," thought Lily, as she walked to the front of the stage and took her final bow.

Dizzy Ballerina Izzy

Izzy loves to ballet dance, like lots of little girls.
She practises every day. She spins and jumps and twirls!
Izzy likes the music, and the pretty costumes, too.
But twirling is her favourite thing. It's what she loves to do.

But though she twirls so beautifully, she has a problem, too:
"I can't tell my left foot from my right! Whatever can I do?"
When all the pretty ballerinas start dancing to the right,
Izzy dances to the left. It happens every night!

"Watch where you are going!" cried Ballerina Di.
"You keep treading on my toes, when you go whirling by!"
Ballerina Zoe said, "She really has to go.
Unless she learns left and right, she's going to spoil the show!"

"I give up!" poor Izzy sobbed, and ran off then to hide.
"I wish I knew my left and right. What can I do?" she cried.
"Don't be upset," said kindly Di. "I know what to do,
To help you solve the problem. Just give me your right shoe."

She tied a bell on to the toe, and fixed it with a stitch.
"When you hear it tinkle, you'll know which foot is which!"
"How wonderful!" cried Izzy, twirling to the right.
"Now I know which one is which, I'd love to dance tonight!"

So Izzy wore her special shoe. Her twirling stole the show!
"Now I can twirl up on the stage and know which way to go!"

Cats and Dogs

Hoddley, poddley, puddle and fogs,
Cats are to marry the poodle dogs;
Cats in blue jackets and dogs in red hats,
What will become of the mice and the rats?

I Bought an Old Man

Hey diddle diddle,
And hey diddle dan!
And with a little money,
I bought an old man.
His legs were all crooked
And wrong ways set on,
So what do you think
Of my little old man?

Hearts

Hearts, like doors, will open with ease
To very, very, little keys,
And don't forget that two of these
Are "I thank you" and "If you please".

New Hay

Willy boy, Willy boy,
Where are you going?
I will go with you,
If that I may.
I'm going to the meadow
To see them a-mowing,
I am going to help them
Turn the new hay.

Two Little Dogs

Two little dogs
Sat by the fire
Over a fender of coal-dust;
Said one little dog
To the other little dog,
If you don't talk, why, I must.

Mother Shuttle

Old Mother Shuttle
Lived in a coal-scuttle
Along with her dog and her cat;
What they ate I can't tell,
But 'tis known very well
That not one of the party was fat.

The Key of the Kingdom

This is the key of the kingdom:
In that kingdom is a city,
In that city is a town,
In that town there is a street,
In that street there winds a lane,
In that lane there is a yard,
In that yard there is a house,
In that house there waits a room,
In that room there is a bed,
On that bed there is a basket,
A basket of flowers.

Flowers in the basket,
Basket on the bed,
Bed in the chamber,
Chamber in the house,
House in the weedy yard,
Yard in the winding lane,
Lane in the broad street,
Street in the high town,
Town in the city,
City in the kingdom:
This is the key of the kingdom.
Of the kingdom this is the key.

Ten Green Bottles

Ten green bottles, standing on a wall,
Ten green bottles, standing on a wall,
And if one green bottle should accidentally fall,
There'd be nine green bottles, standing on a wall.

Nine green bottles, standing on a wall,
Nine green bottles, standing on a wall,
And if one green bottle should accidentally fall,
There'd be eight green bottles, standing on a wall.

Eight green bottles, standing on a wall,
Eight green bottles, standing on a wall,
And if one green bottle should accidentally fall,
There'd be seven green bottles, standing on a wall.

Seven green bottles, standing on a wall,
Seven green bottles, standing on a wall,
And if one green bottle should accidentally fall,
There'd be six green bottles, standing on a wall.

(continue with six green bottles, etc.)

As I Was Going to St Ives

As I was going to St Ives,
I met a man with seven wives.
Each wife had seven sacks,
Each sack had seven cats,
Each cat had seven kits.
Kits, cats, sacks and wives,
How many were going to St Ives?

I Saw Three Ships

I saw three ships come sailing by,
Come sailing by, come sailing by;
I saw three ships come sailing by,
On New Year's Day in the morning.

And what do you think was in them then,
Was in them then, was in them then?
And what do you think was in them then,
On New Year's Day in the morning?

Three pretty girls were in them then,
Were in them then, were in them then;
Three pretty girls were in them then,
On New Year's Day in the morning.

And one could whistle, and one could sing,
And one could play on the violin –
Such joy there was at my wedding,
On New Year's Day in the morning.

The Case of the Carnival Crasher

Molly was going to be a majorette in the village carnival. But there was bad news. "I'm sorry," said Mrs Ellis, the majorette coach. "Our batons have disappeared. We can't practise today."

That evening, Molly's dad came home early from his brass band rehearsal. "Someone has stolen some instruments!" he said. "If we don't get them back, there won't be any music for the parade. The carnival will have to be cancelled."

The next day, Molly went to see Mrs Ellis. "Have you found our batons yet?" she asked.

"I'm afraid not, Molly," Mrs Ellis replied.

As Molly turned to leave, she saw a trophy sitting on a shelf. It was last year's Carnival Queen trophy, and it belonged to Mrs Ellis's daughter, Susie. Molly picked it up.

"Don't touch that!" said Susie, walking into the room.

"Susie is very proud of her trophy," said Mrs Ellis. "But she's got to give it away soon. The new Carnival Queen will want it."

"If the carnival happens,

that is," muttered Susie under her breath.

Molly overheard what Susie said. "I wonder...?" she thought to herself. "Perhaps this is why everything's been going missing!"

"Er... may I use your bathroom please, Mrs Ellis?" asked Molly. She ran upstairs and crept into Susie's bedroom.

Molly spotted a pile of batons under the bed. Something shiny was sticking out of a cupboard. Molly opened the door, and a trombone fell out.

Molly went downstairs holding the trombone and a baton. "Are these yours, Susie?" she asked.

Susie burst into tears. "I wanted to be the Carnival Queen for ever," she cried. "That's why I wanted to stop this year's carnival. I'll make it up to everyone, I promise!"

"You certainly will, Susie!" said her mum crossly.

Susie sniffed loudly. "I know," she said. "I could do face-painting for all the children in the parade."

"Well, that's a start," said her mum.

Susie's face-painting was a huge success. Just before the parade started, Susie presented her trophy to Tiffany, the new Carnival Queen. "Congratulations!" she said. "It's good being a queen, but it's even more fun being a make-up artist!"

Black Beauty Grows Up

The first place I can remember was a large meadow at Birtwick, where I lived with my mother. She always said to me, "I hope you will grow up to be gentle and good."

When I was four years old, my master broke me in. He was a good, kind man. He taught me to wear a saddle and bridle, and to carry a rider on my back. Then I learnt to wear a harness, and to pull a carriage. I had iron shoes fitted to my feet. They did not hurt, but they made my feet feel very heavy.

One day in May, a man came from Squire Gordon's to take me to his home, Birtwick Park. I was put into a pleasant, airy loose-box, next to a fat little grey pony, who said his name was Merrylegs. Beyond him was a tall chestnut mare called Ginger.

She looked cross. There was a stable lad called James, and the coachman who looked after us was called John Manly. He and the Squire were very pleased with me.

Mrs Gordon decided to call me Black Beauty. On Sundays we were turned out in the paddock, and Ginger told me how cruelly she had been treated in her early life. "I never had anyone, horse or man, who was kind to me," she said. It had made her restless and bad-tempered but, as the weeks passed, John Manly's patient and gentle handling made her happier.

One day in the orchard, I asked an old brown hunter called Sir Oliver how he had lost his tail. "It was cut off," he said, "right through the bone, and now I cannot brush the flies away."

"Why did they do it?" asked Ginger.

"For fashion!" said the old horse, with a stamp of his foot. "Fashion is one of the wickedest things in the world."

Soon after this, my master and mistress decided to visit friends who lived forty-six miles away. We stopped overnight at a hotel. Ginger and I were well looked after, but I woke up in the night feeling

very uncomfortable.
The stable was full
of smoke. I heard a
soft, rushing noise,
and there was a
low crackling and
snapping sound. It
made me tremble
all over.

A stable boy burst
in with a lantern and
tried to lead the horses out,
but we were all too terrified to
move. Then I heard James's voice, quiet and cheery. "Come on,
Beauty, we'll soon get you out of this."

He wrapped his scarf round my eyes, and patting and
coaxing led me out of the stable. Then he darted back for
Ginger. I gave a shrill whinny, and Ginger told me later it had
given her the courage to follow me outside. We were led away
from the burning building and spent the rest of the night in the
stables at another hotel.

When we returned home,
we heard that James
was going to a new job.
His replacement was
going to be a young lad
called Joe Green.

A few days later, John woke me in the middle of the night, and rode me at top speed to the town to fetch the doctor, for our mistress was seriously ill. I galloped as fast as I could, and became very hot, but the doctor had to ride me back again, as his own horse was exhausted.

When we got home my legs shook. I was wet through with sweat, and could only stand and pant. Joe gave me a bucketful of cold water, and some food, and left me. Soon I turned deadly cold, and ached all over.

After a long while I heard John's footsteps outside the stable.
He had walked home from the doctor's. I moaned with pain.

John was horrified. He covered me with a soft blanket and gave me warm gruel to drink.

I was ill for many days, and John was very cross with Joe. When he was told Joe had only treated me that way out of ignorance, John exclaimed, "Ignorance is the worst thing in the world next to wickedness."

I often thought of these words when I came to know more of the world.

Little Husband

I had a little husband,
No bigger than my thumb;
I put him in a pint pot
And there I bade him drum.
I gave him some garters
To garter up his hose,
And a little silk handkerchief
To wipe his pretty nose.

The Robins

A robin and a robin's son
Once went to town to buy a bun.
They couldn't decide on a plum or plain,
And so they went back home again.

The Merchants of London

Hey diddle dinkety, poppety, pet,
The merchants of London they wear scarlet;
Silk in the collar and gold in the hem,
So merrily march the merchant men.

The Dame of Dundee

There was an old woman,
Who lived in Dundee,
And in her back garden
There was a plum tree;
The plums they grew rotten
Before they grew ripe,
And she sold them
Three farthings a pint.

Christmas Eve

On Christmas Eve I turned the spit,
I burnt my fingers, I feel it yet;
The little cock sparrow flew over the table,
The pot began to play with the ladle.

Gingerbread Men

Smiling girls, rosy boys,
Come and buy my little toys:
Monkeys made of gingerbread,
And sugar horses painted red.

Egg Raiders

Zac and Lili lived in a nature reserve on Karlin Island. They loved living there. They had lots of fun and some brilliant adventures.

"Do you want to come with me to see the gannets?" Mum asked Zac and Lili one day.

"Yes, please!" they said together.

Gannets were rare sea birds that lived on Black Rock, a small craggy island nearby.

"I hope some of the eggs have hatched," said Lili, as they sailed over to Black Rock. "I can't wait to see the chicks!"

As soon as they had landed, Zac and Lili ran off to the other side of the island.

Suddenly, Zac grabbed Lili's arm. "Look at those men!" he said, pointing.

Lili looked. "Oh no! They're stealing the gannet eggs!" she gasped.

"We can't let them get away," said Zac. "We have to do something."

Zac started running towards the beach. "If we let their boat go they can't escape. Come on, Lili!" he called.

Lili followed him. They both ran as fast as they could.

They found the thieves' boat, moored on the beach.

It was difficult to untie the knot but at last they managed it. Lili and Zac watched the boat float away, and then went to tell Mum what was happening.

"Good work," she said, when she heard what they had done. Then she phoned the coastguard and told him about the thieves.

"I'll be right there," he said. "Leave those thieves to me."

The thieves were looking for their boat when the coastguard arrived.

"You two had better come with me," he said sternly, taking the eggs off them.

When the gannets saw the men being taken away, they started making loud calls.

"I think they're pleased the men are gone!" said Lili.

"Or maybe they're saying thank you – to you!" said Mum.

Mary Had a Little Lamb

Mary had a little lamb,
Its fleece was white as snow,
And everywhere that Mary went
The lamb was sure to go.

It followed her to school one day,
Which was against the rule;
It made the children laugh and play
To see a lamb in school.

Song of the Stars

We are the stars which sing,
We sing with our light.
We are the birds of fire
We fly over the sky,
Our light is a voice.
We make a road for spirits,
For the spirits to pass over.
Among us are three hunters
Who chase a bear;
There never was a time
When they were not hunting.
We look down on the mountains.
This is the song of the stars.

In the Tree-top

Rock-a-bye, baby, up in the tree-top!
Mother his blanket is spinning;
And a light little rustle that never will stop,
Breezes and boughs are beginning.
Rock-a-bye, baby, swinging so high!
Rock-a-bye!

When the wind blows, then the cradle will rock.
Hush! now it stirs in the bushes;
Now with a whisper, a flutter of talk,
Baby and hammock it pushes.
Rock-a-bye, baby! Shut, pretty eye!
Rock-a-bye!

Mother Hubbard

Old Mother Hubbard went to the cupboard
To get her poor doggy a bone;
But when she came there the cupboard was bare,
And so the poor doggy had none.

She went to the tailor's
To buy him a coat
But when she came back
He was riding a goat.

She went to the cobbler's
To buy him some shoes,
But when she came back
He was reading the news.

She went to the hosier's
To buy him some hose
When she came back
He was dressed in his clothes.

The dame made a curtsey,
The dog made a bow,
The dame said, "Your servant,"
The dog said, "Bow wow."

Shy Ballerina Di

Ballerina Di was as dainty as can be.
No other ballerina danced as daintily as she.
When she skipped with other girls, holding hands together,
They said she danced as lightly as a cloud or floating feather!

One day, the teacher told the class, "There's going to be a show.
I want to give the leading role to dainty Di, you know."
"I'm far too shy!" protested Di, "I'd really rather not,
Already, I feel nervous – my tummy's in a knot!"

No matter what the others said, Di firmly shook her head.
"I think the teacher ought to choose someone else instead!"
So Zoe got the leading part, to nervous Di's relief
(Though Di did feel a little disappointed underneath).

Shy Ballerina Di

Everybody practised hard, to learn their ballet parts.
Until all the dancers knew at last every step by heart!
Finally, the first night came, but then disaster struck.
Zoe fell and hurt her foot. It really was bad luck!

"You can't dance the leading part. Whatever shall we do?
Shy Di is the only one who knows the part like you!"
Shy Di looked at all her friends. "I'll dance the part," she sighed.
"I can't let my friends down. At least I will have tried!"

She trembled as the curtain rose, but as the music played,
Di could not believe it! "I just don't feel afraid!"
Di danced as she had never danced. The crowd all called for more.
"What a dainty dancer! She's a star, for sure!"

Little Kitten

Snuggle up, kitten, warm in your bed.
Let moonlit dreams fill your head.

The little bunny curled up tight,
Dreams of carrots every night.

The baby mouse dreams in his nest,
Of cheese, the food that he loves best.

Shut your eyes, kitten, sleep and dream,
Of balls of wool, and bowls of cream.

Mr Moon will guard your bed.
Good night, sleep tight, sleepyhead!

Cuddly Kittens

Five little pussy cats, playing near the door,
One ran and hid inside and then there were four.

Four little pussy cats, underneath a tree,
One heard a doggie bark and then there were three.

Three little pussy cats, thinking what to do,
One saw a tiny bird and then there were two.

Two little pussy cats, sitting in the sun,
One tried to catch his tail and then there was one.

One little pussy cat, looking for some fun,
Saw a pretty butterfly and then there was none.

Five little pussy cats, snuggled in a heap,
They've had a very busy day, but now they're fast asleep!

Smoky the Dragon

Smoky the dragon lived next door to Emma. Every day, Emma went to primary school and Smoky went to dragon school. And every day after school, Emma and Smoky played together. The best game was when Smoky breathed smoke from his nose. He could do lots of clever smoke tricks.

But one day after school, Smoky didn't want to play. He started to cry. "I don't like school," he sniffed. "All the other dragons are clever. They can light fires and boil kettles and even make toast! I can only breathe smoke from my nose."

Emma hugged Smoky, but she didn't know what to say.

The next day it was Emma's birthday party. Marvo the magician was coming to do some magic tricks.

Halfway through the birthday tea the phone rang.

"Oh dear," said Mum when she got off the phone. "Marvo's ill. He won't be able to come. I don't know what to do."

"We can do clever tricks," said three of the dragons. "We can boil kettles and light fires and make toast!"

"They aren't party tricks," said Mum.

"Smoky can do lots of clever smoke tricks," said Emma.

So Smoky made smoke curl and swirl and made smoke rings to jump through.

"What a clever dragon!" said Mum.

And Smoky smiled a big smoky smile!

A Tiger for Tara

It was Saturday morning. Tara was very excited. She was going to the pet shop to buy a pet.

"What pet shall we buy?" asked Mum, on the way to the pet shop.

"Let's buy a hippo," said Tara.

"Oh, no," said Mum. "A hippo is too fat."

"Let's buy an elephant," said Tara.

"Oh, no," said Mum. "An elephant is too big."

"Let's buy a snake," said Tara.

"Oh, no," said Mum. "A snake is too long and wiggly."

Outside the pet shop was a boy with a toy tiger. "I definitely want to buy a tiger," said Tara. "A tiger would be the best pet."

Inside the pet shop there were big pets and small pets, fat pets and thin pets. But there were no tigers at all.

"These pets are good," said Tara. "But a tiger would be better."

"We can't have a tiger," said Mum. "They are too fierce."

"Wait here," said the pet shop owner. He went into the back room and came back out with a basket of kittens. There were black and white kittens and one small stripy kitten.

"This kitten's name is Tiger," said the owner. "Would you like him as a pet?"

"Oh yes!" said Tara. She gave Tiger a hug. "Tiger is the best pet of all."

Man Overboard!

Zac and Lili had been to the mainland with Dad to fetch supplies. They boarded the ferry to sail home to Karlin Island.

Dad found a friend to chat with so Zac and Lili went off to look around.

"Be careful," Dad shouted after them.

"We will," they promised. Zac and Lili headed up to the deck so they could look out for dolphins.

"Look at that little boy, Zac," Lili gasped, pointing. "That's so dangerous."

A young boy was sitting on the top of the ferry rail.

Suddenly, the ferry hit a large wave and tipped to the side. The boy slipped and fell into the sea.

Lili and Zac rushed over to the rail.

"Help!" the boy shouted, waving his arms. "I can't swim!"

"I'll throw him the life belt," Zac told Lili. "You go and tell the captain to stop the ferry."

Lili ran off towards the captain's cabin shouting for help. Zac lifted the life belt off its hook and tossed it to the boy. The boy stretched out his arms and grabbed it.

"Hold tight!" Zac called. "Lili's gone to get help. You'll soon be out of there." Zac knew it was important for the boy to keep calm.

The ferry stopped moving. Zac smiled. Fast work, Lili!

The captain came hurrying over, with Lili, Dad and the boy's worried parents.

"I'll lower the lifeboat," the captain said.

Dad offered to row the lifeboat.

"Careful, Dad!" cried Lili anxiously. "The waves are big!"

Dad rowed carefully out to the boy and pulled him into the lifeboat.

Before long the boy was back on board, wrapped in a blanket.

"Thank you for saving me," the boy said to Lili and Zac. "I'll never sit on the rail again!"

The Wedding

Pussycat, wussicat, with a white foot,
When is your wedding and I'll come to it.
The beer's to brew, and the bread's to bake,
Pussycat, wussicat, don't be too late.

First

First in a carriage,
Second in a gig,
Third on a donkey,
And fourth on a pig.

Gee Up, Neddy

Gee up, Neddy,
Don't you stop,
Just let your feet go
Clippety clop.
Clippety clopping,
Round and round.
Giddy up,
We're homeward bound.

Slowly, Slowly

Slowly, slowly, very slowly
Creeps the garden snail.
Slowly, slowly, very slowly
Up the garden rail.

Quickly, quickly, very quickly
Runs the little mouse.
Quickly, quickly, very quickly
Round about the house.

Hark! Hark!

Hark, hark,
The dogs do bark,
Beggars are coming to town:
Some in rags,
Some in tags,
And some in velvet gowns.

The Little Bird

This little bird flaps its wings,
Flaps its wings, flaps its wings,
This little bird flaps its wings,
And flies away in the morning!

My Little Puppy

Everyone agreed that Isobel's little puppy, Patches, looked adorable. He had stumpy legs and a round, chubby tummy, silky-soft ears, lively brown eyes and a small patch just over his right eye.

Isobel loved Patches and Patches loved Isobel.

The only problem was that Patches was always getting himself – and Isobel – into trouble.

Lots of trouble!

On Monday, Patches chewed one of Dad's slippers… and the strap on Mum's new handbag.

"Can't that animal chew on his toy?" complained Dad.

"He doesn't like it," sighed Isobel, trying to give Patches the rubber bone she had bought for him. Patches put his paws on Isobel's hands and licked them.

"That tickles," giggled Isobel. It was impossible to be cross with Patches for long.

On Tuesday, Patches pulled the clothes off the washing line and dragged them through the soil. The clothes were all dirty.

"Oh, Patches, not again!" complained Dad.
"He was only trying to play," defended
Isobel. "He's really sorry, aren't you,
Patches?"

Patches barked and
rolled over on his back,
waving his legs in the air.
Even Dad had to laugh.

On Wednesday, Patches
knocked over a vase.

"He was only trying to smell the flowers," said Isobel.
Patches put his head on one side and barked softly.

"See," said Isobel. "He's saying 'sorry,' aren't you, Patches?"
Mum grinned. "All right, but be more careful!"

Later that day Mrs May, who lived next door, was in her
garden. Her white cat, Snowy, jumped on top of the fence and
hissed at Patches.

Patches barked back.

"Please don't let that naughty puppy frighten
poor Snowy," called Mrs May.

"We'll make sure Patches stays out
of Snowy's way," said Mum.

"Yes, please do," sniffed
Mrs May. "Poor Snowy!"

"Poor Snowy, indeed,"
muttered Isobel. "That cat is
always teasing Patches."

"Now, now, Isobel," soothed Mum. "Mrs May was telling me earlier that she's lost her gold ring. I think her husband gave it to her a long time ago. She's very upset about it, and that probably makes her seem more cross than she really is. And you know she loves Snowy as much as you love Patches."

Mum was right. Mrs May and Snowy were best friends.

The next day Isobel and Patches were in the garden with Mum and Dad when Mrs May came out of her house.

"Any sign of your ring?" called Mum. Mrs May shook her head sadly. "I think I've lost it for good," she said.

Just then, Snowy jumped down from the fence, scratched Patches across his nose with her paw, then ran off.

"Snowykins!" cried Mrs May. "Naughty puss!"

Patches squeezed through a hole in the fence and began to chase Snowy round and round Mrs May's garden. Isobel and her parents followed. Round and round they went – till Dad caught Patches.

"Oh, no! Look at my vegetables!" cried Mrs May. "And my poor flowers!"

"We're so sorry," said Isobel's mum. "We'll help you replant them."

"That would be very kind," said Mrs May.

Mum and Mrs May picked up the plant pots and the gardening tools. Dad tied together the runner-bean canes that had been knocked over. And Isobel and Patches dug holes to put back some of the flowers that had been disturbed.

"What's that, Patches?" asked Isobel, as Patches pushed a lump of soil towards her with his nose. Isobel scraped away the soil, then leaped to her feet.

"Mrs May! Mrs May! Patches has found your ring!"

Mrs May was delighted. "Oh, you clever puppy!" she said, patting Patches' head. "How can I ever thank you?"

And after that, Isobel, Patches and Mrs May were the best of friends.

Even though Patches still sometimes chased naughty Snowy round and round the garden!

Dolphin Finds a Star

One night in the moonlight, a baby dolphin called Splash looked up and saw a shooting star. It zoomed across the sky and disappeared.

"That star has fallen into the water!" Splash cried. "I'm going to find it and give it to my mummy as a present. She loves shiny things."

In the distance Splash saw something sparkling. He swam towards the sparkles, thinking it was the star.

But when he got closer, he saw that it was a shoal of flashing fish, wiggling and weaving through the water.

Then Splash saw something glowing above his head. "There's the star! My mummy will be so pleased," he thought happily, and he swam towards the shining light.

But when he got closer, Splash found that the light was a lamp shining on the very top of a sailing boat.

The more the baby dolphin swam around, the more shiny creatures he saw. There were flashing fish, jiggly jellyfish and even sparkly seahorses, but the fallen star was nowhere to be found.

At last, Splash saw a light that was much brighter than all the rest.

in the hair of a beautiful mermaid queen sitting on her throne.

"Hello, baby dolphin. What brings you here?" she asked, but Splash felt very shy. He didn't know what to say.

So the flashing fish, the jiggly jellyfish and the sparkly seahorses all told the mermaid queen:

"He was looking for the star that's in your hair. He wanted to give it to his mummy."

"In that case, you shall have it," said the mermaid, and she handed the shining star to Splash.

Splash gave his mummy the star and she was very pleased.

Together they played with it all day long.

Then, when night came, they jumped up as high as they could and pushed the star back up into the sky, where it could shine down on everyone – on the flashing fish and the jiggly jellyfish, on the sparkly seahorses and on you, too.

What a Bad Goat!

Farmer Jim was doing his rounds to see all the animals on the farm.

Pig was looking after her ten piglets. "What a good pig!" said Jim.

Hen was laying a big brown egg. "What a good hen!" said Jim.

Horse was eating a bale of hay. "What a good horse!" said Jim.

Cow was being milked. "What a good cow!" said Jim.

Duck was swimming on the pond. "What a good duck!" said Jim.

Cat was chasing mice. "What a good cat!" said Jim.

Dog was watching the farm gate. "What a good dog!" said Jim.

Jim went back to the farmhouse. "I wonder where Goat is?" he said to himself. Then he saw! Goat was in the farmhouse garden eating the washing. He had already eaten six socks, and he was starting on a dress.

Jim chased Goat away from the washing line. "What a bad goat!" he said.

Silly Pig

One day, Pansy Pig decided to go and look for treasure.

"You silly pig!" said the other animals. "You won't find treasure on the farm."

First, Pansy saw a sparkling necklace in the tree.

"Treasure!" she said. "I shall put it round my neck."

But the sparkling necklace wasn't really a necklace. It was a spider's web sparkling with raindrops.

Spider was very angry. "You silly pig!" she said.

Pansy saw some red earrings in the hedge.

"Treasure!" she said. "I shall put them on my ears."

But the red earrings weren't really earrings. They were red berries.

Blackbird's nest was next to the red berries. She was very angry. "You silly pig!" she said.

Then Pansy saw something sparkling in the mud.

"Treasure!" she said. And this time... it really was treasure!

Farmer Kate was in the farmyard.

"Hello, Pansy!" she said. "What have you got there?" She took the treasure.

"You've found my ring!" said Kate. "You clever pig!"

Beach Rescue

Zac and Lili were worried. They hadn't seen their favourite dolphin, Whistler, for a while.

"Dolphins sometimes swim quite far out to sea," Mum told them. "I'm sure Whistler will be back soon."

But there was no sign of Whistler the next day. Or the next.

"What if something has happened to him?" said Lili.

"Can we go and look for him, Dad?" begged Zac.

"Okay," Dad agreed. "But I'm sure he's fine."

They all set off in Dad's boat.

After a while, they saw some dolphins ahead.

"Let's get a bit closer and see if Whistler is among them," said Dad. They looked and looked but Whistler was nowhere to be seen.

Now Lili and Zac were really worried. Where was Whistler?

To their surprise the dolphins started to surround the boat. They whistled and leaped in the air. They swam away for a bit and then came back again.

"I think they want us to follow them, Dad!" said Zac.

"You may be right!" agreed Dad.

The dolphins led them to a nearby island. As they got closer, Lili saw another dolphin lying on the beach.

"It's Whistler!" she shouted. "He must be injured!"

Dad moored the boat and they all ran over to Whistler.

"What happened to him?" asked Zac.

"He must have swum too close to the island, then got stranded when the tide went out," Dad explained. "If we don't get him back into the sea soon, he will die," he added quietly.

"Oh no!" cried Lili and Zac.

"We must keep Whistler wet until Dolphin Rescue arrive," he said.

They fetched buckets from the boat and began pouring seawater over Whistler.

At last, Dolphin Rescue arrived. Carefully they helped Whistler back into the sea.

The dolphin swam off. Then he leapt out of the water with a big splash and clicked happily.

"I think he's saying thank you to us for saving him!" laughed Dad.

"Bye, Whistler!" called Lili.

Sam Duckling Swims

Sam Duckling lived by the pond with Mummy Duck and the other ducklings.

"Jump in and swim," said Mummy Duck one day. *Splash!* All the little ducklings jumped in and swam – except Sam.

"Jump in and swim," said Mummy Duck. "It's fun!"

Sam put his wing into the water. "The water's too cold," he said. "And it looks very deep. I'll stay here."

"Quack! Quack!" quacked the other ducklings. "Swim with us, Mummy! Swim with us!"

Mummy Duck went off to swim with the other ducklings, leaving Sam all alone on the bank. He began to cry.

Just then Frog popped his head out of the water. "Hello, Sam," he said. "I'll help you swim."

Frog got a lily pad. "Sit on the lily pad, Sam," he said. Sam sat on the lily pad and Frog pulled Sam along.

"Now splash your feet," said Frog. Sam splashed his feet.

"This is fun!" quacked Sam.

"Now get off the lily pad," said Frog. Sam got off the lily pad.

"I'm swimming!" he cried.

"Well done!" quacked Mummy Duck.

Lost in the Jungle

One summer, Poppy and her mum and dad went on a jungle safari for their holiday.

Poppy packed a map and compass.

"You won't need a map and compass," said Dad. "We're going to a part of the jungle where there are special paths to follow."

Poppy still packed her map and compass.

When they arrived in the jungle, Poppy got out her map and compass. "We're here," she said, putting a big cross on the map.

"We don't need a map and compass," said Dad. "Follow me!" They climbed into their jeep and went deep into the jungle. At a crossroads a sign said, 'To the pool'.

"We're going north," said Poppy.

"Great!" said Dad.

Soon they came to the pool. Poppy looked at her map. "We're here," she said, putting another cross on the map.

They took lots of photographs of the animals at the pool. Then Dad said, "Time we went back to camp."

They went back along the path, but when they got to the crossroads the sign had gone.

"Don't worry," said Poppy. "We can follow my map."

Soon they were back at the camp. "You were right, Poppy," said Dad, laughing. "We did need a map and compass."

What Do You Think?

There was an old woman, and what do you think?
She lived upon nothing but victuals and drink:
Victuals and drink were the chief of her diet;
This tiresome old woman could never be quiet.

The Baby in the Cradle

The baby in the cradle
Goes rock-a-rock-a-rock.
The clock on the dresser
Goes tick-a-tick-a-tock.

The rain on the window
Goes tap-a-tap-a-tap,
But here comes the sun,
So we clap-a-clap-a-clap!

A Cat Came Fiddling

A cat came fiddling out of a barn,
With a pair of bagpipes under her arm;
She could sing nothing but, "Fiddle cum fee,
The mouse has married the bumble-bee."
Pipe, cat – dance, mouse,
We'll have a wedding at our good house.

Bobby Shaftoe

Bobby Shaftoe's gone to sea,
Silver buckles at his knee;
When he comes back
He'll marry me,
Bonny Bobby Shaftoe!

Dance to Your Daddy

Dance to your daddy,
My little babby;
Dance to your daddy,
My little lamb.

You shall have a fishy,
In a little dishy;
You shall have a fishy
When the boat comes in.

Teeth

Thirty white horses upon a red hill,
Now they tramp, now they champ,
Now they stand still.

Black Beauty's New Owners

I had been living happily at Squire Gordon's for three years when we were told that because the Squire's wife was ill, she would have to leave England to live in a warmer country. The grey pony Merrylegs was given to Mr Blomefield, the vicar, and Joe went to look after him. Ginger and I were sold to an earl, who lived in a very grand house called Earlshall Park.

John, Squire Gordon's coachman, told the new coachman, Mr York, all about us. The following day we were harnessed to the carriage to take out the lady of the house, and our heads were held up unnaturally high with bearing reins.

When we had to go up a steep hill I could not put my head forward and pull the carriage up as usual, but took all the strain on my back and legs. I began to dread having my harness put on, and Ginger said, "I can't bear it, and I won't."

Each day our heads were reined up tighter. One day Ginger reared up and kicked right over the carriage pole, then fell down, kicking me as she did so.

We were both sore and bruised. Ginger was never put in the carriage again and I had a new partner called Max.

In the spring the family went to London. They left a groom, Reuben Smith, in charge of the horses. One day he drove me to town in the carriage to get it repaired, and was to ride me home. He left me at an inn, and got back very late. The stable boy said I had a loose shoe, but Reuben took no notice and set off at a gallop. My shoe came off, and still he galloped, over roughly laid sharp stones.

My foot split and, in terrible pain, I stumbled and fell on both knees, throwing Smith off.

After many hours some men from the house came out to search for us. They found us and led me slowly home. In time, my knees healed, but they were badly scarred. Ginger, too, had been injured by hard riding. She was to be rested, but I was to be sold. My owner said, "I cannot have knees like that in my stables."

I went to a livery stable as a 'job-horse'. This meant I could be hired out to anyone who wished to drive me. Many people had no consideration for me at all, and treated me as if I were an engine.

One day a good driver hired me, and I was sold to his friend, Mr Barry. But his groom left the stable dirty, and I got an infection in my feet. After this I was sent to a horse fair to be sold again.

There are all kinds of horses and ponies at a horse fair, and all kinds of buyers. Some are very rough, but a small, gentle, cheery man said to me, "Well, old chap, I think we should suit each other."

He bought me and rode me home, and I became a London cab horse.

My new owner, Jerry Barker, had his own cab. An old war-horse called Captain did the morning work, and I did the afternoons. We worked hard, but our master treated us well and we had a day of rest every Sunday.

One bitterly cold New Year's Eve, our passengers kept us waiting for hours and, when we got home, Jerry became ill with a bad cough and a fever. He almost died and had to give up cab work, and so I was sold again.

It was then that began the most dreadful period of my life.

I Hear Thunder

I hear thunder, I hear thunder
Hark don't you? Hark don't you?
Pitter patter raindrops, pitter patter raindrops,
I'm wet through. So are you!

I see blue skies, I see blue skies,
Way up high, way up high.
Hurry up the sunshine, hurry up the sunshine,
We'll soon dry! We'll soon dry!

Getting Dressed

We're going out to play, but first we must get dressed!
I'll start by looking for my cosy white vest.
I need to find my pants now. They're my favourite – spotty red!
I wonder where they are… Oh! They're right here on my bed!

Where's my yellow T-shirt? I can't see it anywhere.
I'll look inside my wardrobe… Yes! It's hanging there!
Next, my denim trousers – I saw them just last night!
I left them on the chair, I think… Yes! They're here, I'm right.

Now if only I could find my socks then I could put them on!
My red socks should be in the drawer… where have they gone?
Okay, now I've found my socks then I can put on shoes,
I've got two pairs right by my bed – which ones shall I choose?

I'll need my warm green sweater that's made of fluffy wool,
I've found it in my toybox – all I have to do is pull!
I've got my coat – I'm ready! But there's one thing left to do.
I'll have to dress my teddy. Oh! Looks like Teddy's ready too!

Showy Ballerina Zoe

Ballerina Zoe could leap high off the ground,
And land so very gracefully, she'd barely make a sound!
But though she was so graceful, it went right to her head.
Instead of practising her steps, she used to boast instead.

It made the other dancers cross. "We're quite fed up with Zoe.
Why does she have to brag so much, and be so proud and showy?"
One day, Zoe had some news: "I've heard about a show.
There's going to be an audition. I think we all should go!

I know that I will win a part. Of that, you can be sure.
But you might get a little role, if you would practise more."
The day of the audition came. "I'll stretch and do some bends,
To warm up ready for the test," said Zoe to her friends.

But as she stretched her tutu ripped. The others heard it tear!
"What shall I do?" Zoe cried. "I've nothing else to wear."
"Don't worry!" Dizzy Izzy cried. "We'll dance around you.
Then no one else will ever see the big hole in your tutu!"

So Di and Izzy twirled about, with Zoe in between.
Zoe was delighted. "We make a splendid team!
Now each of us has won a part, it's very plain to see,
Not only are you great friends, you can dance as well as me!"

Rock Pool Friends

Sid the seahorse was playing hide-and-seek with his friends on the coral reef.

"Three... two... one..." he counted.

Suddenly, there was a whooshing noise. *Splash!* A big wave crashed over the reef and tumbled him over and over.

When Sid stopped tumbling, he opened his eyes. Everything looked strange. "This isn't a reef," he decided. "It looks like a rock pool."

He sat on a shiny shell to decide what to do, feeling lonely.

"Do you mind?" snapped a voice inside the shell. "You're sitting on my house." It was a little hermit crab called Katy.

"Sorry," said Sid. "I didn't think anyone lived here."

Katy clicked her claws loudly. "It's safe to come out!" she cried. All at once, orange starfish, pink shrimp, red crabs, yellow and green sea anemones and shimmering fish appeared.

"Wow!" gasped Sid. "Your home is just as colourful as my home on the coral reef." Then he sighed a little sigh.

"What's the matter?" asked Katy.

"Do you think I'll ever see my home again?" asked Sid.

"Of course you will," smiled Katy. "You just need to catch a wave. The tide is going out. If you hurry you'll get a ride at once."

"Bye, bye, everyone," cried Sid, as a wave carried him off.

"Bye, Sid! Come back any time," shouted Katy.

And that's exactly what Sid did!

The Flyaway Fairy

One day, some little fairies were learning to
fly. Poppy, Fern and Rosie were very good,
but Daisy was scared of falling.

"I don't want to fly," she whispered.

Daisy's best friend was Caterpillar.
"Can you teach me to fly?" she asked him.

"I don't have any wings," said Caterpillar.
"But I'm sure someone will help."

Caterpillar took Daisy to see Bumblebee.

"Will you teach me to fly?" asked Daisy.

"Buzz buzz! Sorry! I don't have time!" Bumblebee replied.
"I'm too busy collecting nectar from the flowers."

So Caterpillar took Daisy to see his friend Bluebird.

"Can you teach me to fly?" asked Daisy.

"I'm sorry, I'm afraid I can't leave my chicks," replied Bluebird.
It seemed that no one wanted to teach Daisy to fly.

But a few days later Daisy got a big surprise. She was
sitting on a flower feeling sorry for herself when a beautiful
creature fluttered towards her and called out, "Hello, Daisy!
It's me... Caterpillar! I've changed into a butterfly.
Now that I have wings I can teach you to fly.
It's easy!"

Daisy's friend taught her to fly in no time.

"Now I know how to do it, I don't feel
scared any more," Daisy laughed.

347

Stranded

Dad had to check on some seal pups near Black Rock, so Lili and Zac went with him.

"They're so cute," said Lili, smiling.

"They're all fit and healthy too," said Dad, looking pleased.

They set off home again to Karlin Island, but they hadn't gone very far when Zac noticed water swishing around his feet. "Dad! The boat's leaking!" he shouted.

Lili looked. "The water's coming in fast, too!" she gasped. "It must be a big hole!"

Dad quickly fetched a bucket. "Let's try and bale the water out," he said. "I'll head back to Black Rock."

But the water was coming in too fast. Soon it was almost up to Lili's knees.

"Dad! The boat's sinking!" she cried.

"Don't panic. Look, we're almost there," said Dad, pointing to the craggy island not far ahead. "We can swim the rest of the way."

They jumped overboard in their life jackets, and swam through the sea.

"I'll phone for help," Dad said when they were

safely on Black Rock. But his mobile phone had disappeared. "Oh no! It must have fallen out of my pocket into the sea," he groaned.

Lili and Zac were cold, wet and miserable.

"Don't worry, Mum will come looking for us soon," Dad told them.

"But how will she know where to find us?" asked Lili.

Dad thought about that. "We'll light a fire," he decided. "When Mum sees the smoke she'll come to find out what's going on."

They collected some dry branches and twigs, and Dad rubbed two twigs together to spark the fire to life.

They all huddled around the fire to keep warm.

Before long Lili spotted a motorboat chugging towards them. It was the coastguard.

Then they heard a familiar voice coming through the coastguard's loudhailer. It was Mum!

"Need some help over there?" she asked.

"Hooray!" cheered Zac loudly.

"We'll soon be home now," said Dad.

Polar Bear and the Rainbow

Ben, the little polar bear, was the same colour as snow. He was the same colour as his sister and his mum.

He was the same colour as polar bears everywhere.

"How boring," thought Ben.

Ben watched the sunrise with his friends, the hare and the fox. "You look pink in the new sunlight," they told him.

"I'm pink! I'm pink!" cried Ben. But as the sun climbed higher he turned back to the colour of snow.

Ben went swimming with his friend the seal.

"You look blue in the water," she told him.

"I'm blue! I'm blue!" cried Ben. But when he climbed out of the water he turned back to the colour of his sister and his mum.

That night, Ben dreamt that he was as bright and sparkly as a rainbow. But when he woke up his rainbow fur had gone.

The next day, Ben found a snowman. He had a big smile made of stones.

"The snowman is the same colour as me, and he looks very happy," thought Ben.

Then Ben played hide-and-seek with his friends.

"The snow is the same colour as me. That's why I'm good at hide-and-seek," thought Ben.

Soon sparkly white snowflakes began to fall all around. The snowflakes felt tingly on Ben's nose.

"Snowflakes are the same colour as me, and they are beautiful," thought Ben.

At the end of the day, Ben cuddled up with his family.

"I don't mind being polar bear-coloured after all. I am the same colour as snowmen and snowflakes," he thought.

Best of all, he was the same colour as his sister and his mum. They were soft and snuggly, like polar bears everywhere, and he loved them very much.

Give Me a Hug!

Missy was a very daring little mouse. She liked to swing from willow branches... until one day she fell off!

Then Missy didn't feel daring at all. She stumbled back home to her mum.

"Give me a hug!" wailed Missy.

"Of course I will," said Mum. She stroked poor Missy's aching head and, very quietly, she said, "How's that? Does that take away the pain? Here's a hug to help you feel better again." Then she hugged Missy tight.

And Missy did feel better. Missy was a very cheerful little mouse. She smiled as she helped. She hummed as she played. But one day, when Missy lost her favourite teddy, she didn't feel cheerful at all. She ran downstairs to her mum.

"Give me a hug!" wailed Missy.

"Of course I will," said Mum.

She told Missy to look under the bed, and when Missy found Teddy there, Mum gently said, "I knew you'd find Teddy. You see, I wasn't wrong. Have a hug and I don't think those tears will last long." Then she hugged Missy tight.

And Missy began to smile. Missy was a very brave little mouse. She liked to sneak up to the farm cat and tickle his whiskers.

That night, though, Missy heard noises under the bed. And she didn't feel brave at all. She crept along to her mum's room.

"Give me a hug!" wailed Missy.

"Of course I will," said Mum.

After Mum had given Missy a hug she took Missy back to her room and looked under the bed. Then, as she tucked Missy in, Mum smiled and said, "Missy, I've looked and I promise you there's nothing there."

One morning when Mum was really very busy, Missy came running into the room.

"Give me a hug!" she pleaded.

"What's happened now?" asked Mum. Missy smiled. "Nothing! It's just... your hugs make me happy!"

"That's good," said her mum, "because I like it when you ask me if I'll hug you. Our hugs are the best thing, and I love them too!"

A Thorn

I went to the wood and got it;
I sat me down and looked at it;
The more I looked at it the less I liked it;
And I brought it home because I couldn't help it.

Cross Patch

Cross patch,
Draw the latch,
Sit by the fire and spin;
Take a cup,
And drink it up,
Then call your neighbours in.

Baa, Baa, Black Sheep

Baa, baa, black sheep, have you any wool?
Yes, sir, yes, sir, three bags full;
One for the master, one for the dame,
And one for the little boy that lives down the lane.

I Love Little Pussy

I love little pussy, her coat is so warm;
And if I don't hurt her she'll do me no harm.
So I'll not pull her tail nor drive her away,
But pussy and I very gently will play.

Pussycat Mole

Pussycat Mole,
Jumped over a coal,
And in her best petticoat
Burnt a great hole.
Poor pussy's weeping,
She'll have no more milk,
Until her best petticoat's
Mended with silk.

On the Grassy Banks

On the grassy banks
Lambkins at their pranks;
Woolly sisters, woolly brothers,
Jumping off their feet,
While their woolly mothers
Watch them and bleat.

Brave Little Deer

Deer woke up on a bright summer morning. She found Bear hunting for honey.

"Would you like to play?" asked Deer.

"I'm sorry," replied Bear, "but I haven't had breakfast yet. Help me get this honey, and then I can play."

"Oh, Bear!" sighed Deer. "The buzzing bees scare me."

"Well, then you'd better watch out," Bear told her. "There's a wolf about!"

Deer set off through the woods. "If only I was as brave as Bear," she thought, "I'd have someone to play with."

Suddenly Deer heard a cry. "Help! Help!" called a frightened voice. Deer started to rush towards it.

"Someone's in trouble!" she called, as she passed Bear.

"Sorry," said Bear. "It might be that wolf. I'm scared of wolves."

In a clearing was Rabbit, shivering as the wolf snarled at him.

Deer didn't stop to think. She leapt between the wolf and Rabbit. As she did so, her hoofs hit a hollow log. Boom! The sound echoed through the wood and the wolf fled.

"Oh, thank you, Deer!" smiled Rabbit. "You were so brave. I don't know anyone else who would have done what you did."

"Thank you," said Deer shyly. "I don't suppose you have any time to play, do you?"

"Of course!" said Rabbit.

Kind Little Bear

Little Bear, Squirrel and Bunny were going out to play.
"Don't go into the river," said Bunny's mum.

"And don't get dirty," said Squirrel's mum.
Bear and his friends played all
morning. At last, Squirrel and Bunny
flopped down in the long grass near the
river. But Bear wasn't tired at all!
"I'm so thirsty!" gasped Bunny.
"I'll get you a drink," smiled Bear. He
splashed into the river and scooped up water in his
big paws.

"I'm so hungry," groaned Squirrel.

"I'll fetch you some nuts," smiled Bear. He scrambled up a
nearby tree, getting twigs and leaves stuck in his wet fur.

"Goodness," sighed Bunny's mum, when they got home.
"You're soaking wet, you naughty bear. You've been in the river!"

"Just look at your dirty fur, you naughty bear!" said
Squirrel's mum.

"I was thirsty, so Bear went into the river to get
me a drink," said Bunny.

"Bear got dirty getting me some nuts," added
Squirrel.

Bunny's mum and Squirrel's mum smiled.
"You're not a naughty bear at all," they said.
"You're a kind little bear!"

I Love You, Grandma

Little Bear and Grandma were eating breakfast.

"Grandma," asked Little Bear suddenly, "why do I have such sharp claws?"

"To help you find food," came the reply.

"But you told me I have my nose for that," said Little Bear, surprised. "You told me to sniff the air."

"Ah!" said Grandma. "Sometimes your nose leads you to food, but you still have to work to get it."

She took Little Bear to the woods. "Sniff the air!" she reminded him.

Little Bear started to follow his nose. He stopped at a fallen tree.

"I can smell food," Little Bear said. "I can't see it, but I know it's here."

"You'll need to use your claws," Grandma told him. Little Bear dug his sharp claws into the bark. He broke off a small piece.

"Ants!" he laughed. "Delicious!"

"Lunch," smiled Grandma. "Good work, Little Bear!"

"Grandma," asked Little Bear suddenly, "why do I have such a long tongue?"

"To help you find food," Grandma said at once.

"But you told me that I have my nose and claws to do that,"

said Little Bear, surprised.

"Sometimes the best food is hard to reach," Grandma said. She took Little Bear to a clearing. "Smell the air," she said. Little Bear sniffed hard. He lifted his nose.

"Food!" he told Grandma. A huge bees' nest hung from a branch above him.

"I know what to do," laughed Little Bear. He hooked the nest with his sharp claws, lifted it down, and opened it up.

"Honey!" he smiled. "Mmmmm!"

"Supper," said Grandma. But Little Bear's big claws couldn't reach the food.

"So what are you going to do now?" asked Grandma.

"Use my long tongue," laughed Little Bear. And he did!

"How do you know so many things, Grandma?" asked Little Bear suddenly.

"That's easy," Grandma smiled. "When I was small, I was curious... just like you," she said. "You ask so many questions, you'll soon know lots of things, too." And she hugged Little Bear tight.

"Do you know I love you, Grandma?" asked Little Bear.

"I do!" answered Grandma. She stroked Little Bear's sticky head. "And you know I love you, too," she said.

My Little Kitten

Ella went to visit her grandma every weekend.

Grandma's house was very pretty, with roses growing around the front door and a big garden at the back.

It was also full of cats. Lots of cats.

There was Lady Jane, a white and brown cat with very fluffy fur. There was Duchess, a bluish-grey cat with large pointed ears and tiny oval paws. And there was Ella's favourite, Princess Mae, a creamy-coloured tabby cat with short, soft fur.

Ella loved to help Grandma look after the cats.

First, her grandma would give the cats their food. Each cat had its own special bowl. Then Ella helped Grandma to groom them. Lady Jane and Duchess needed their long hair brushing at least once every day.

Princess Mae could lick her own fur clean because it was much shorter. But she still loved to sit on Ella's knee, purring softly, while Ella combed her creamy coat.

Sometimes Grandma entered her cats in special cat competitions.

They had won lots of prizes. Ella loved to look at all the photographs and trophies on Grandma's mantelpiece. Her favourite was a large gold cup.

One weekend, Grandma had some exciting news. Princess Mae was going to have kittens!

"Would you like to choose one of Princess Mae's kittens for your very own?" asked Grandma.

"Oh, yes, please," gasped Ella, with shining eyes.

"You'll have to be patient," said Grandma. "The kittens won't be here for another month or so, and then they'll have to stay with their mum until they are around ten weeks old."

Ella's face fell. "Do I really have to wait that long?" she asked.

"I know that seems like a long time, but it will fly by," said Grandma. Ella nodded glumly.

One day, Ella went round to help her grandma prepare for the new arrivals. They had bought a basket and covered it with an old blanket.

"Princess Mae can have her kittens in here," explained Grandma. "It's warm and dry, and she'll feel safe."

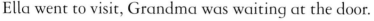

Princess Mae seemed to know at once that the basket was for her.

The next time Ella went to visit, Grandma was waiting at the door.

"I've got something to show you," she said, smiling. "Princess Mae's kittens have arrived!"

Ella and Grandma crept quietly into the kitchen. There, curled up beside Princess Mae, were five tiny, furry kittens.

"They were born last night," whispered Grandma.

"They're beautiful!" said Ella softly. "When can I pick one?" she whispered.

"Whenever you like," replied Grandma, "but it's best to wait until they are older, then you'll know for sure which one you want."

At first, the kittens spent most of their time curled up next to Princess Mae, drinking her milk or sleeping.

Then, after a week or so, they began to crawl. One stripy little kitten crawled right across the floor to sniff Ella's hand.

After two weeks, the kittens began to explore.

Ella was at her grandma's baking some cakes when the same stripy little kitten came over and tried to join in.

When they were four weeks old, the kittens began to grow teeth. The stripy little kitten especially loved playing with the red chewing toy that Ella had bought.

By the time the kittens were six weeks old, they were racing around and playing with each other. "I think you've chosen your favourite," smiled Grandma one day as she watched Ella playing with the stripy kitten.

"I think she's chosen me," laughed Ella. "I'm going to call her Tiger Mae – after Princess Mae and because she's stripy! And do you think I could enter Tiger Mae in cat competitions when she's older?"

"Yes," replied Grandma, smiling. "You've learned a lot about looking after cats. I think that would be a very good idea!"

"Do you hear that, Tiger Mae?" whispered Ella. "Maybe one day we'll win a big gold cup, too."

And just a little while later… they did!

Lucky Little Duck

Duck was waddling through the meadow when she met Bunny.

"Hello, Bunny," said Duck.

Just at that moment, something sparkly darted past Duck's head.

"Wow!" said Duck. "Did you see that? It was beautiful! What was it?"

"I'm going to find out," laughed Bunny, hopping off towards the pond.

"Lucky Bunny," sighed Duck sadly, as she waddled after him. "Look at his strong legs. I could never move that fast."

They could soon see the mysterious creature darting round and round above the pond. Then it settled on a tall reed. Duck slipped into the water and paddled quietly towards it.

"Lucky little Duck," sighed Bunny. "I can't swim at all."

"Wow!" whispered Duck, as she reached the reeds. Perched on the tallest reed was the most beautiful creature she had ever seen. Its wings sparkled in the sun. Its body shimmered blue and green.

"Hello," said Duck. "I'm Duck."

"I'm Dragonfly," replied the creature.

"Come and meet my friend Bunny," said Duck. She swam back to the bank.

"We're both lucky – because we have a new friend!" she said to Bunny.

Shy Little Bunny

Bunny's whiskers twitched excitedly as he poked his nose out of his family's new burrow.

"Why don't you see if you can meet some new friends, Bunny?" said his mum.

Bunny scampered off to explore. Soon he heard some voices nearby. He peered through the brambles to see a mouse, a duck and a squirrel building a den.

"Help me push in this stem, Mouse," said a young duck.

"I am pushing, Duck!" said the mouse.

"I'll help, too," said a young squirrel.

Duck, Mouse and Squirrel stood back to look at their work.

"It's a good den," said Squirrel, "but it would be better if it had a burrow in it."

Bunny hopped out from behind the brambles. "I'm good at burrowing," he said shyly.

"Really?" said Duck. "Could you help us?"

So Bunny dug a hole inside the den. Then he scooped out a tunnel. Finally, he made a snug little burrow inside.

"Wow!" cried Squirrel.

"The fox will never get in there!" said Mouse.

And Bunny played happily with his new friends outside their new den all day long.

Pussycat, Pussycat

Pussycat, pussycat, where have you been?
I've been up to London to visit the Queen.
Pussycat, pussycat, what did you there?
I frightened a little mouse under her chair.

Silly Sally

Silly Sally swiftly shooed seven silly sheep.
The seven silly sheep Silly Sally shooed shilly-shallied south.
These sheep shouldn't sleep in a shack;
Sheep should sleep in a shed.

Rock-a-bye, Baby

Rock-a-bye, baby, thy cradle is green;
Father's a nobleman, Mother's a queen,
And Betty's a lady and wears a gold ring,
And Johnny's a drummer and drums for the King.

There Was an Old Woman

There was an old woman lived under a hill,
And if she's not gone she lives there still.

Frisky Lamb

A frisky lamb
And a frisky child
Playing their pranks
In a cowslip meadow:
The sky all blue
And the air all mild
And the fields all sun
And the lanes half-shadow.

Frog Went a-Courtin'

Mr Froggie went a-courtin' an' he did ride;
Sword and pistol by his side.
He went to Missus Mousie's hall,
Gave a loud knock and gave a loud call.

"Pray, Missus Mousie, air you within?"
"Yes, kind sir, I set an' spin."
He tuk Miss Mousie on his knee,
An' sez, "Miss Mousie, will ya marry me?"

Little Lamb

"Baa! Baa!" says Lamb to Mummy Sheep,
"Please can we play hide-and-seek?"

"Where's my lamb?" asks Mummy Sheep.
"Baa! Baa!" shouts Lamb, and out she leaps!

"Baa! Baa!" says Lamb. "I'll hide again –
In the piglets' muddy pen!"

But Mummy finds her right away.
"Baa! Baa!" is all that Lamb can say.

"Baa! Baa!" says Lamb. "I'll hide with my friends."
Mummy says, "There you are with the hens!"

"Baa! Baa!" says Lamb, when the day is done,
"Playing hide-and-seek is fun!"

Little Calf

"Moo! Moo!" says Calf, one sunny day.
"The meadow's where I like to play!"

When a butterfly lands on little Calf's nose,
He says, "Moo! Moo!" and away it goes!

Calf follows the butterfly, calling, "Moo! Moo!"
He sees woolly Lamb and says, "You come too!"

Just then, little pink Piglet appears,
"Moo! Moo!" says Calf. "We're over here!"

As the butterfly flutters off through the air,
Calf says, "Moo! Moo! It's over there!"

Calf snuggles with Mum when his busy day ends.
He says, "Moo! Moo! I've had fun with my friends!"

The Storm

One night, Lili and Zac were woken up by a big storm. Thunder crashed and lightning flashed. It sounded very scary.

"I can't sleep," said Zac, opening the curtains to look.

"Nor me," said Lili. They both went downstairs. Mum and Dad were in the kitchen.

"The storm woke us up," said Zac.

"It's a bad one," agreed Mum. Suddenly the lights went out.

"The electricity's gone off!" cried Lili.

Dad went to fetch some oil lamps. They all sat drinking hot chocolate by lamplight and listening to the storm. Then Dad's phone rang. He looked worried as he talked.

"That was the lighthouse keeper," he said. "The lighthouse

has been struck by lightning. Now it doesn't work."

Dad told them that a boat was trying to come into Karline Island harbour. "It won't be able to see its way without the light from the lighthouse," he said. "We'll all have to take some searchlights and guide it safely in."

They all made their way to the dark harbour. "First we need to find the boat," said Dad. He shone his big searchlight out to sea. "There it is!" he pointed.

"Oh no!" gasped Mum. "It's heading for the rocks!"

They all stood together and shone the searchlights to guide the boat into the harbour. The boat didn't change direction.

"It's still heading for the rocks!" shouted Zac.

They watched the boat in dismay. Would it see their lights in time?

Then slowly, the boat started to turn around.

"It must have seen us!" Lili yelled excitedly.

The boat followed the searchlights safely into the harbour.

When the captain got out, he came straight over to them.

"Thank you so much," he said. "I don't know what would have happened if you weren't here."

"No problem!" said Lili proudly.

Black Beauty Finds a Home

After the kindly cab driver Jerry had to sell me because he had fallen ill began the most terrible part of my life.

First I went to a carter, who overloaded me and wore me out. Then he sold me to a dreadful cab driver called Skinner, who worked his horses until they could work no more. Every day, with no day off to rest, I pulled overloaded cabs, and got whipped for not working hard enough when I was doing my best. At night I was too exhausted to eat, and I felt so utterly wretched I wished my life would end.

Then one day it nearly did. With four people and a mountain of luggage to haul uphill, and me thin and weak from overwork, my feet slipped from under me. I fell heavily to the ground on my side. I thought I was dying.

"He'll never get up again," I heard someone say. But cold water was thrown over me and eventually I staggered to my feet.

Skinner was persuaded to rest me for a few days, then sent me to another sale. Here I was put with the old, broken-down horses.

A man and a young boy came and looked at me. "There's a horse, Willie, that has known better days," said the man, patting me on the neck.

"Could you not buy him, Grandfather, and make him young again?" asked the boy.

I trotted out as well as my poor, stiff legs would allow. They bought me, took me home, fed me hay and oats, and gave me the run of the meadow in the daytime. By the spring I was so much better that they could drive me a few miles, and I did the work with perfect ease.

One day I was groomed with special care and driven to a pretty house near the village. Three ladies, the Misses Blomefield, were to take me on trial.

When their groom was cleaning me next morning, he said, "That is just like the star

Black Beauty had. And here's the knot in his skin where he was bled, and the little patch of white hair on his back! Why, it must be Black Beauty! Don't you know me? It's little Joe Green, who almost killed you when you were a young horse!" But Joe was a grown man now.

I was driven out each day, and I have now lived in this happy place a whole year. The ladies have promised I shall never be sold, so I have nothing to fear. Often, in the mornings, before I am quite awake, I fancy I am still in the orchard at Birtwick where I grew up, standing with my old friends under the apple trees.

Bye Baby Bunting

Bye baby bunting,
Father's gone a-hunting,
To fetch a little rabbit-skin
To wrap his baby bunting in.

Hush-a-bye, Baby

Hush-a-bye, baby, on the tree-top,
When the wind blows the cradle will rock;
When the bough breaks the cradle will fall,
Down will come baby, cradle and all.

A Star

I have a little sister, they call her Peep, Peep;
She wades the waters deep, deep, deep;
She climbs the mountains high, high, high;
Poor little creature she has but one eye.

Nothing-at-all

There was an old woman called Nothing-at-all,
Who rejoiced in a dwelling exceedingly small;
A man stretched his mouth to its utmost extent,
And down at one gulp house and old woman went.

There Was an Old Woman Had Three Sons

There was an old woman had three sons,
Jerry and James and John:
Jerry was hung, James was drowned,
John was lost and never was found,
And there was an end of the three sons,
Jerry and James and John!

Old Mother Goose

Old Mother Goose,
When she wanted to wander,
Would ride through the air
On a very fine gander.

I Love You, Mummy

"Look at me, Mummy," called Little Bear. "I'm going to pick those fruits."

"Just a minute," replied Mummy Bear. "There's something you might like to know."

But Little Bear was already climbing the tree.

Mummy Bear saw Little Bear run along a branch.

She saw Little Bear reach out his paw to pick a juicy fruit.

Then Little Bear began to wibble and wobble... *Crash!*

"This doesn't feel like fun!" thought Little Bear.

"Not bad!" said Mummy Bear. "But you look at me now, Little Bear. I'll show you how to climb properly before you go fruit-picking again."

Little Bear watched how Mummy balanced as she climbed.

"Your turn now, Little Bear," she said. Little Bear did what Mummy Bear had done.

"This tastes good!" thought Little Bear. "I love Mummy."

"Look, Mummy," smiled Little Bear. "All the other cubs are playing. I'm going to play, too."

"Wait a minute, please," said Mummy Bear. "There's something you might like to know."

Little Bear stopped and turned. "Tell me," he said.

"Be gentle when you play," said Mummy Bear. "Like this." Mummy Bear reached out her paws. She wrapped her arms round Little Bear and rolled him over and over on the ground.

"I love Mummy," thought Little Bear. Then he ran off to play. He did just what Mummy Bear had done. And it felt like fun.

Little Bear was very tired when he got home, but there was something he wanted to say.

"I wanted to tell you," said Little Bear.

"What?" asked Mummy Bear.

"I love you, M…"

But Little Bear didn't finish.

Mummy Bear kissed Little Bear's sleepy head.

"I love you, too," she said.

Lost at Sea

"I'm off to take some photos of basking sharks," said Mum one morning. "Do you two want to come with me?"

"Yes, please!" said Lili and Zac together. They grinned at each other.

Mum fetched her camera, and then they all got into the boat and set off.

Zac was first to spot the basking sharks. "There they are!" he pointed.

"Look at that one. It's leaping!" gasped Lili.

Zac and Lili loved watching the sharks.

Mum took lots of photos. "I can't wait to go home and print them out," she said happily.

But Mum had been so busy following the sharks she'd gone too far out to sea. "Never mind, I'll soon find the way home," she told Lili and Zac.

Then it started to get foggy. The fog came down so thick it was hard to see in front of them.

"Oh dear, I think we're lost," said Mum.

Some whistles and squeaks sounded out nearby. Dark shapes bobbed about in the water, at the side of the boat, whistling loudly.

"Dolphins," said Mum.

The dolphins swam round the boat, whistling and leaping out of the water.

"What are they doing?" asked Zac.

"I think they want to show us the way home," said Mum. "I've heard stories of dolphins helping people lost at sea."

Then they heard a familiar clicking sound.

"Whistler!" shouted Lili. Whistler was their favourite dolphin.

Whistler kept very close to the boat. Mum followed him and the other dolphins through the fog until at last Karlin Island nature reserve jetty came into view.

"I think Whistler and his friends guided us home to say thank you for helping him before," Lili said, as they climbed out of the boat.

"I think you're right," agreed Mum.

"You're great, Whistler!" called Zac.

Index